ROBIN

BATMAN ADVENTURES

ROBIN

THE BOY WONDER

CONTENTS

ROBIN

"... AND AFTER HE GOT ME THAT SECOND TIME, THAT'S WHEN I GOT THE BATMAN TATTOO..."
"...FOR HUMILITY."
LIVE BAIT
LENNIE'S
"TO REMIND ME I AIN'T THE TOUGHEST MUG IN THE WORLD."
"...THAT THERE'S ALWAYS SOMEONE TOUGHER."

SPEAKING OF TOUGH... IT'S BEEN REAL TOUGH PUTTING MY HANDS ON MONEY SINCE I GOT OUTTA THE JOINT, BERNIE.
I MIGHT NOT MAKE RENT, KNOW WHAT I MEAN?

YOU WANT I SHOULD HOOK YOU UP WITH SEGARINI AND THE ICEMAN?
DO A COUPLE JOBS?
NO...NO. I WENT STRAIGHT. I LEARNED MY LESSON.
LOVE

IT'S GOOD MONEY, DIXON.
I DON'T WANT MORE JAIL TIME, BEN. IF I BREAK THE LAW I MIGHT RUN INTO HIM...

AND IF I NEVER SEE THIS FACE AGAIN IN REAL LIFE...
...THAT'S ALL RIGHT WITH ME.
HATE

DAGGER'S SECRET
WRITTEN BY: TRIGGER TEMPLETON
PENCILLED BY: BATTLE-AX BURCHETT
INKED BY: BAYONETTE BEATTY
COLORED BY: LAND MINE LOUGHRIDGE
LETTERED BY: HOWITZER HARKINS
EDITED BY: VERBAL ABUSE VINCENZO
EXIT
AW JEEZ...
I GOT TO LEARN TO SHUT MY STUPID MOUTH.

WE'RE HERE FOR TOMMY SILK. NO ONE ELSE.
YOU ARE NOT THE LAW, BATMAN. I DON'T HAVE TO DO A THING YOU SAY.
ISN'T THAT RIGHT, BOYS?
IF YOU KNOW WHAT'S GOOD FOR YOU, THE REST OF YOU WILL KEEP OUT OF THE WAY.
uh-oh... THEY'RE GONNA TRY TO TAKE 'EM. THEY NEVER LEARN...
THEY NEVER LEARN.
I GOT HIM!
ME FIRST!
NORMALLY, I LOVE A GOOD BAR FIGHT...
BUT I DON'T WANT BATMAN HANDING ME ANOTHER BEATING.
SO I'M GONE.

LAST ONE TO KNOCK OUT FIVE BAD GUYS BUYS LUNCH!
HEY BATMAN!
AW, NO... DON'T COME THIS WAY.
WHAM!
THUCK!
HAW HAW! YOU THINK YOU CAN TAKE ME, MIDGET?
SMASH!
huh...?
DAGGER...?
DAGGER DIXON...?
TIM...?

KPOW!!
THANKS FOR DISTRACTING THE RUNT FOR ME, CHIEF. I OWE YOU.
WHAM!
WHAT KIND OF A CREEP ARE YOU?!
HE'S JUST A LITTLE KID!
YOU OKAY...?
MORE OR LESS, THANKS.
CAN I BORROW YOUR SHOULDER FOR A SECOND?
GICK!
huh?
TIME FOR MY PATENTED IMPENETRABLE MIDGET SCISSOR-LOCK GRIP OF DEATH, TOMMY!

KWACK!
WHAM!

BAM!
SMACK!

THOK!
KRACK!

BAD IDEA.
oh...

I GUESS I OWE YOU LUNCH.
I'D INVITE TOMMY HERE TO JOIN US, BUT HE'S A LITTLE TIED UP.

YOU'RE GOING DOWN FOR THE MURDER OF BUTCH VON BULOW, TOMMY.
I'M NOT SAYING A THING.
YOU DON'T HAVE TO, YOUR PRINTS WERE ALL OVER THE POCKET WATCH.

DAGGER DIXON, ISN'T IT? I SAW YOU HELP ROBIN THERE.
GOOD TO SEE YOU STAYING ON THE RIGHT SIDE OF THE LAW SINCE YOU GOT OUT.
YEAH... I KEEP STRAIGHT...

BEEN DOING A LITTLE OF THIS AND THAT...
...SEEING OLD FRIENDS...

MAKE SURE IT'S THE RIGHT KIND OF FRIENDS, DIXON. I'LL BE KEEPING AN EYE ON YOU.
COME ALONG, TOMMY...
HEY!

OH YEAH... IT'S THE RIGHT KIND OF FRIEND, ALL RIGHT.
I WANT A LAWYER, BATBREATH!
I'M NOT THE LAW, TOMMY... I DON'T HAVE TO DO A THING YOU SAY.

HEY! DEADBEAT! YOU'RE TWO WEEKS BEHIND WITH THE RENT.
I'M NOT CARRYING YOU BUMS ANYMORE. ONE MORE WEEK AND YOU'RE OUT.
SHUT YOUR HOLE, SLAPPY... I'M WORKING ON IT.
NO EXCHANG ON LOST MONEY
NO CREDIT
OFFICE
EXIT
MOLDOFF ARMS
I'M CALLING SOMEONE WHO'S CONNECTED RIGHT NOW...
BILLIONAIRE ADOPTS AGA
YEAH, HELLO.
IS TIM DRAKE THERE?
YES, SIR... JUST ONE MOMENT, PLEASE.
BET YOU DIDN'T EXPECT TO BE HEARING FROM YOUR OLD PAL DAGGER, DID YA?
DAGGER...?
UM... WHAT MADE YOU THINK OF CALLING ME AFTER ALL THIS TIME?

OKAY... WE PLAY IT THAT WAY.

I JUST GOT OUT OF JAIL, I'M CATCHING UP. YOU AND ME ARE STILL BEST PALS, RIGHT?

LIKE YOUR *DAD* AND ME WERE *PARTNERS*, WE WATCHED EACH OTHER'S BACKS...

...TWO-FACE NEVER COULD HAVE GOT HIM IF I'D BEEN WITH HIM THAT NIGHT.

BUT I WATCH OUT FOR *YOU TOO*, SPORT. REMEMBER? ALWAYS.

YEAH. YOU'RE THE ONLY ONE OF DAD'S FRIENDS THAT WAS EVER NICE TO ME. I REMEMBER...

SO THE THING IS... I NEED MONEY, TIM, AND IT LOOKS LIKE YOU LUCKED INTO SOME WHILE I WAS AWAY...

THAT'S NOT MY MONEY, DAGGER! THAT'S BRUCE'S... I CAN'T GIVE YOU ANY...

LOOK, WE BOTH KNOW I KNOW SOMETHING ABOUT YOU, YOU'D RATHER KEEP QUIET, RIGHT?

THAT'S GOTTA BE WORTH SOMETHING.

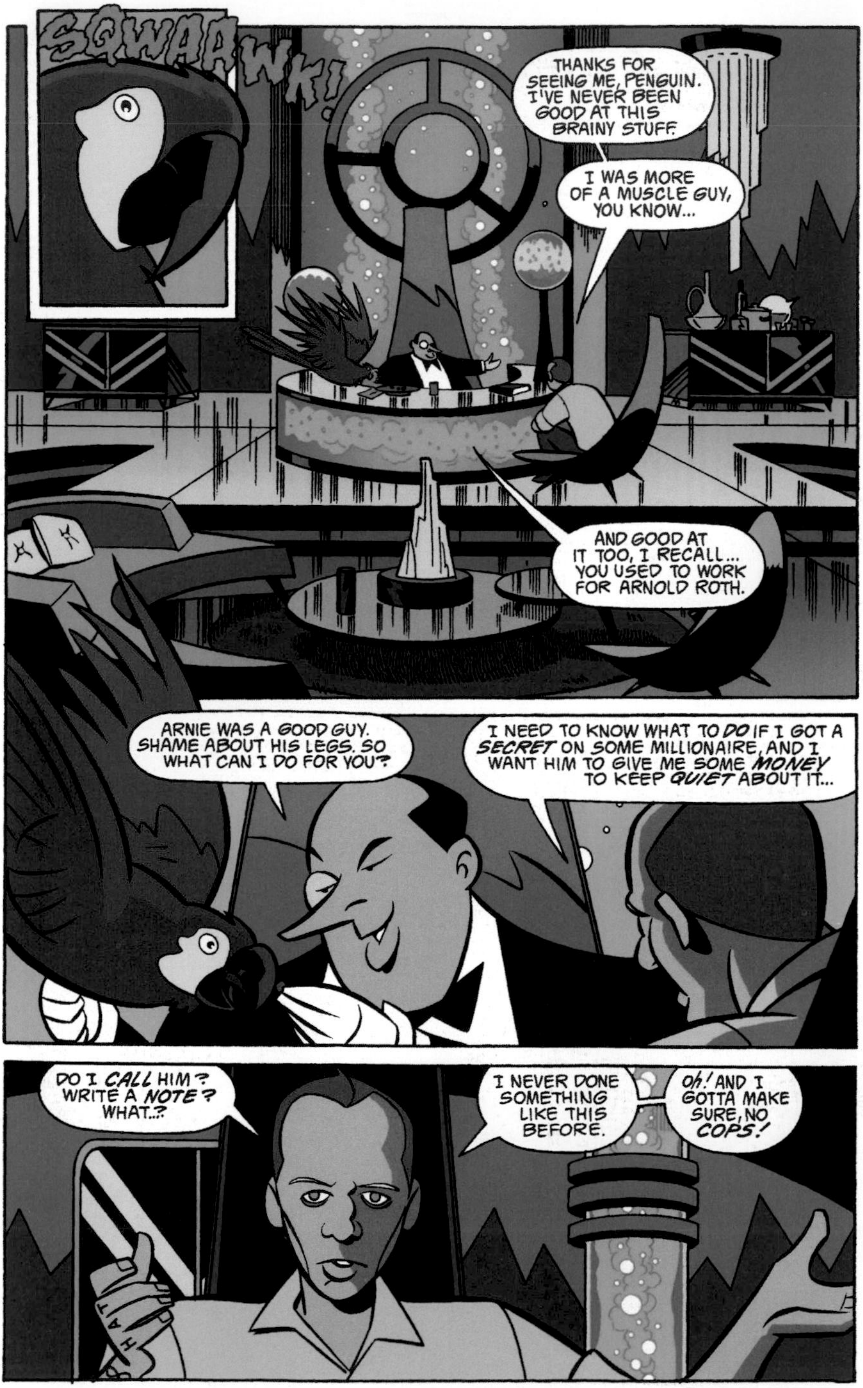

SQWAAWK!
THANKS FOR SEEING ME, PENGUIN. I'VE NEVER BEEN GOOD AT THIS BRAINY STUFF.
I WAS MORE OF A MUSCLE GUY, YOU KNOW...
AND GOOD AT IT TOO, I RECALL... YOU USED TO WORK FOR ARNOLD ROTH.

ARNIE WAS A GOOD GUY. SHAME ABOUT HIS LEGS. SO WHAT CAN I DO FOR YOU?
I NEED TO KNOW WHAT TO *DO* IF I GOT A *SECRET* ON SOME MILLIONAIRE, AND I WANT HIM TO GIVE ME SOME *MONEY* TO KEEP *QUIET* ABOUT IT...

I CAN HELP YOU BETTER, MR. DIXON, IF YOU TELL ME WHAT THIS PARTICULAR PIECE OF INFORMATION IS, AND ABOUT WHOM...
Uh... NO CAN DO, MR. PENGUIN. IT'S A SECRET, RIGHT?

COME NOW, COME NOW... NO NEED TO BE COY, WE'RE ALL FRIENDS HERE.

Nah, SORRY, THIS IS BETWEEN HIM AND ME.
I COULD CUT YOU IN FOR SOME OF THE MONEY IF YOU HELP ME PLAN IT OUT, THOUGH...
THIRTY PERCENT... NO RISK TO YOU... JUST TELL ME HOW TO SET IT UP, IS ALL.

THAT'S ***QUITE*** A SURE THING IF YOU'RE WILLING TO OFFER UP THAT KIND OF A PERCENTAGE ***JUST*** FOR SOME ***ADVICE***.
UNDER THESE CIRCUMSTANCES, I REALLY MUST ***INSIST*** YOU TELL ME WHAT YOU KNOW.
SNAP!

YOU'LL NEED SOME FOR YOUR FACE, JERK!
THOK!
CRASH!
WAAUUGH! HE WAS FAKING!

THINK, DIXON, *THINK!*
THE PENGUIN KNOWS WHO YOU ARE. HE COULD FIND THAT FLOPHOUSE YOU'RE STAYING AT IN NO TIME.
CAN'T GO THERE.

AND AFTER PASTING TOMMY SILK IN THE FACE LIKE THAT, I CAN'T HAVE MANY FRIENDS LEFT AT LENNY'S...

I NEED TO SEE *TIM*.

YEAH.

ONLY BATMAN AND ROBIN CAN HELP ME NOW.
HEY...I'M TRYIN' TO SLEEP HERE!

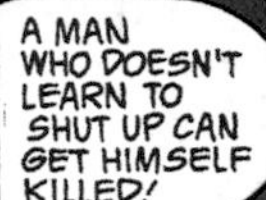

A MAN WHO DOESN'T LEARN TO SHUT UP CAN GET HIMSELF KILLED!

KNOCK KNOCK

MY WORD!

YOU GOTTA LET ME SEE TIM. I GOTTA TALK TO TIM.
JUST A MOMENT, SIR, AND I'LL SEE IF HE'S AVAILABLE. ARE YOU ALL RIGHT?

I'LL BE ALL RIGHT AS SOON AS YOU LET ME SEE TIM. OUTTA MY WAY, POPS!
AND I SAID I *WILL* SEE IF HE'S AVAILABLE. ONE SIMPLY CANNOT BARGE IN HERE LOOKING AS YOU DO...
PLEASE DON'T FORCE ME TO RESTRAIN YOU...

I'D LIKE TO SEE YOU TRY, YOU LIMEY BEANPOLE. YOU'LL BE...
IT'S ALL RIGHT, ALFRED...

I KNOW HIM.
...HE'S A FRIEND.

I ALREADY TOLD YOU, I CAN'T GIVE YOU ANY MONEY, DAGGER. WHAT ARE YOU DOING HERE?
I DON'T NEED MONEY RIGHT NOW. I NEED YOU TO PROTECT ME!
WHAT...? ME...?

DON'T PLAY DUMB. I KNOW WHO YOU ARE.
I SAW YOU GET THIS BRUISE LAST NIGHT FROM TOMMY SILK.

I... I WALKED INTO A DOOR...
YEAH, RIGHT. AND I'M A POLAR BEAR.
I KNOW WHO YOU ARE. I NEED YOU AND BATMAN TO PROTECT ME. YOU GOTTA...
LOVE

LOOK... I DID SOMETHING STUPID. I TOLD THE PENGUIN I KNEW SOMETHING ABOUT SOMEBODY... SOMETHING BIG! BUT I DIDN'T SAY WHAT.
AND NOW HE'S GONNA KILL ME TO TRY TO FIND OUT WHAT IT WAS.

IF THEY CATCH ME, THEY'RE GOING TO GET IT OUT OF ME, I'M NOT THAT STRONG.
PENGUIN WILL FIND OUT WHO YOU REALLY ARE, AND HE'LL KILL YOU, TIMMY. I CAN'T EVER LET THAT HAPPEN.

YOU'RE SHIFTY'S BOY. I PROMISED HIM I'D ALWAYS DO GOOD BY YOU.
BUT I DON'T KNOW WHAT TO DO... I NEED HELP...

EXCUSE ME, SIR... ARE YOU A FRIEND OF MY WARD'S?
BRUCE?
UM... YEAH... THIS IS CHARLIE DIXON... A FRIEND OF MY FATHER'S, ACTUALLY.

WELL, THEN, MR. DIXON. IT'S LATE ON A SCHOOL NIGHT. PERHAPS IT WOULD BE BETTER IF YOU CAME BACK IN THE MORNING.
IT'S OKAY, BRUCE... I'M HANDLING THIS.

WHY DON'T YOU TELL ME WHAT IT IS YOU'RE HANDLING, AND I'LL DECIDE?
UM... I CAN'T... IT'S A SECRET.

KNOCK KNOCK KNOCK

SMASH!
YOU'RE AS EASY TO FOLLOW AS A BULL ELEPHANT, MR. DIXON.
GOOD EVENING, MR. WAYNE. WHAT AN ODD SURPRISE.

... SO YOU'RE OUR LITTLE MILLIONAIRE, ARE YOU ?
WHAT ARE YOU DOING IN MY HOUSE, COBBLEPOT ?
THIS MAN IS AN EMPLOYEE OF MINE.

HE WALKED OUT OF MY CLUB WITH SOMETHING THAT BELONGED TO ME, SO I'M TAKING STEPS TO --
HE'S LYING! I KNOW YOUR SECRET, MR. WAYNE, AND HE'S TRYING TO BEAT IT OUT OF ME!

MY SECRET...?
I TOLD YOU TO SHUT UP, DAGGER! YOU'RE NOT HELPING!

SECRET...? NONSENSE. SHEER NONSENSE.
HE'S AN EMBEZZLER, I ASSURE YOU.
AND I SHALL DISCIPLINE HIM AS I SEE FIT. YOU'D DO BEST TO KEEP OUT OF THE WAY.

FEEL FREE TO CALL THE POLICE IF YOU WISH.
I OWN MOST OF THEM ANYWAY.

THIS HAS GONE ON LONG ENOUGH...
DON'T SWEAT IT, BRUCE. I'M HANDLING IT.

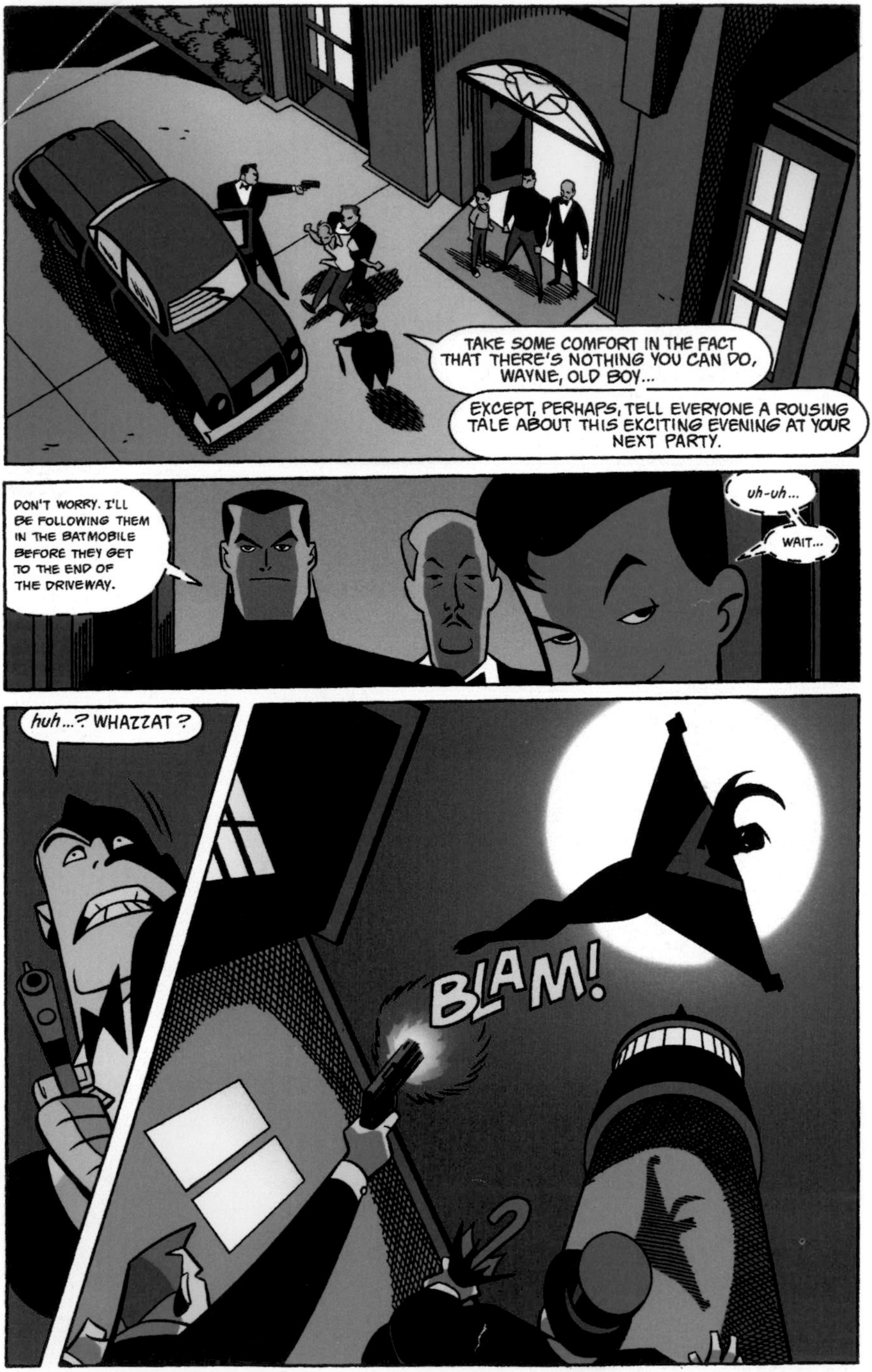

TAKE SOME COMFORT IN THE FACT THAT THERE'S NOTHING YOU CAN DO, WAYNE, OLD BOY...
EXCEPT, PERHAPS, TELL EVERYONE A ROUSING TALE ABOUT THIS EXCITING EVENING AT YOUR NEXT PARTY.

DON'T WORRY. I'LL BE FOLLOWING THEM IN THE BATMOBILE BEFORE THEY GET TO THE END OF THE DRIVEWAY.
uh-uh...
WAIT...

huh...? WHAZZAT?
BLAM!

NIGHTWING WAS WORKING OUT IN THE WEIGHT ROOM IN THE CAVE.
I CALLED HIM ON MY WRIST-COMM THE SECOND PENGUIN WALKED IN.
BOK!
VVAUUGH!
TWACK!
TOLD YA I WAS HANDLING IT.

I'VE BEEN WATCHING YOU ALL NIGHT, PENGUIN... BREAKING AND ENTERING... KIDNAPPING... LOOKS LIKE YOU'RE FINALLY GOING DOWN.
Bah! A MOMENTARY HEADACHE FOR MY LAWYERS, NO MORE.

BUT YOU, DIXON, HAVE A LIFETIME OF LOOKING OVER YOUR SHOULDER. NO MATTER WHERE YOU RUN...
... SOMEDAY YOUR SECRET WILL BE MINE.

HE'S RIGHT. HE'LL GET ME SOMEDAY. NO-WHERE'S SAFE.
I MIGHT AS WELL TELL HIM WHAT I KNOW ABOUT YOU, WAYNE.

DAGGER! WILL YOU *EVER* LEARN TO SHUT UP!
MR. DIXON, PERHAPS YOU AND I SHOULD...

I KNOW SOMETHING ABOUT YOUR YOUNG WARD, HERE...
HE'S GOT A JUVENILE RECORD. SHOPLIFTING AND STUFF... HE EVEN SPENT SOME TIME IN A JUVIE HALL.
HOW WOULD IT LOOK TO YOUR STOCKHOLDERS IF PEOPLE KNEW YOU'D ADOPTED A COMMON STREET THUG?

YOU WEREN'T INTENDING TO BLACKMAIL ME WITH THAT, WERE YOU? THAT INFORMATION WAS WRITTEN UP IN NEWSTIME MAGAZINE.
EVERYONE IN AMERICA WHO READ THAT ISSUE KNOWS ABOUT TIM.
WHA...? IT WAS?

HA HA HA HA!
YOU'RE RIGHT, DIXON! YOU *NEVER* WERE THE BRAINS!
HA HA HA HA HA!

THIS WAY, SIR, YOU'RE IN NEED OF MEDICAL ATTENTION.
I SAID IT JUST LIKE YOU TOLD ME, LITTLE SPORT.
LOOKS LIKE IT WORKED. GREAT IDEA.

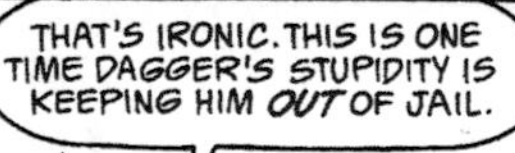
THAT'S IRONIC. THIS IS ONE TIME DAGGER'S STUPIDITY IS KEEPING HIM *OUT* OF JAIL.

YEAH... PRETTY STUPID, *huh?*

SAN DIEGO. THREE WEEKS LATER.
TATTOOS
TACOS
KEEP IT CLEAN, AND RUB HAND CREAM INTO IT FOR THE NEXT TWO DAYS...
YEAH, YEAH... I'VE HAD TATTOOS BEFORE.

I NOTICED. SO WHAT'S THE BATMAN TATTOO FOR? THAT'S A GOOD ONE...
FOR HUMILITY.

BATMAN BEAT ME A FEW TIMES BACK IN GOTHAM. IT'S WHY I AIN'T NEVER GOING BACK.
BUT I LOOK AT THIS ONE EVERY NOW AND THEN TO REMEMBER THAT I AIN'T ALWAYS GONNA WIN EVERY FIGHT NO MATTER WHERE I AM.

SO WHAT'S THE NEW ONE I JUST DID FOR? YOU NEEDED A MATCHING SET?
IT'S A SECRET. THE NEW ONE IS TO HELP ME KEEP SECRETS.

TO REMIND ME WHAT SOMEONE ONCE TOLD ME.
"A MAN DOESN'T LEARN TO SHUT UP, HE CAN GET HIMSELF KILLED."
END!

CHAPTER 2: A LITTLE THING

ROBIN

ROBIN?

Hi, Kids!
Welcome to
Play Zo

A Little Thing!
SCOTT PETERSON-writer
TIM LEVINS-penciller
TERRY BEATTY-inker
LEE LOUGHRIDGE-colorist
TIM HARKINS-letterer
JOSEPH ILLIDGE-associate editor
DARREN VINCENZO-little guy
BATMAN created by BOB KANE

I THINK YOU *GOT* HIM, PARTNER.
HE OKAY, BATGIRL?

HE WON'T BE WINNING ANY BEAUTY CONTESTS ANY TIME SOON.

WHAT WERE YOU THINKING, ROBIN?

YOU JUMP IN THERE WITHOUT A PLAN AND JUST--
SAVE SOME KIDS?

YES. YES, YOU *DID*. YOU SAVED SOME KIDS.
BUT YOU COULD HAVE BEEN KILLED. OR ONE OF THOSE KIDS COULD HAVE BEEN.

WOULD THAT HAVE BEEN WORTH IT?
COULD ANYTHING BE WORTH *THAT*?

NO.
I JUST... I DON'T KNOW. SOMETIMES THIS JOB JUST GETS TO YOU.
WHAT I WOULDN'T GIVE FOR THE GOOD OL' DAYS I'VE HEARD ABOUT.
I'D TRADE JUST ONE OF THESE PSYCHOS WITH A GUN FIXATION FOR A DOZEN COSTUMED VILLAINS ANY DAY.
WE'VE GOT THOSE.
Oh, SURE. TWO-FACE, THE JOKER, BANE.
THOSE GUYS ARE A REAL LAUGH A MINUTE.

YOU KNOW WHAT I'M TALKING ABOUT -- COLORFUL COSTUMES, WACKY CRIMES AND RIDICULOUS MOTIVATIONS.
SOME DOOFUS WHO GETS THE BRIGHT IDEA TO PULL A CRIME BASED ON THE TIDES OR A PASSING COMET OR SOMETHING.
I... I DON'T KNOW.
I GUESS I DON'T REALLY KNOW WHAT I'M LOOKING FOR.
WHAT D'YA THINK?
IT'S WORTH A SHOT.

HEY, BOY WONDER. I JUST PICKED UP A REPORT OF SOMETHING GOING DOWN IN THE DINIVILLE PROJECTS.
MEET YOU THERE.
WHAT'S GOING ON?
TENANTS REPORT SOMEONE LURKING ABOUT. THEY CLAIM IT'S SOMEONE SAYING IT'S TIME FOR PEOPLE--
"--TO REAP WHAT THEY SOW."

COME ON, CHUM! LET'S GET 'ER!

THE OLD ONE-TWO COMBINATION! LET'S SHOW HER HOW WE TAKE CARE OF HER TYPE IN GOTHAM CITY.

COME ON! WHAT ARE YOU WAITING FOR?
WHY WOULD I WANT TO HIT BATGIRL?

Wha?
YOU KNEW?
Oh, PLEASE. LIKE I --
BACKUP REQUIRED AT 325 KAYLEIGH AVENUE. NOW.

WELL, IT LOOKS LIKE BATMAN DIDN'T NEED US AFTER ALL.
DO YOU SUPPOSE HE'S FINISHED?
BAM!
THUD!

YUP.

SORRY TO CALL YOU OUT HERE -- THIS DIDN'T TAKE QUITE AS LONG AS I EXPECTED.
ROBIN, THERE ARE FOUR HOSTAGES IN THE FRONT ROOM. MAKE SURE THEY'RE FINE, THEN DOUBLE-CHECK THE REST OF THE HOUSE.

DO YOU REALLY THINK YOU MIGHT HAVE MISSED SOMETHING INSIDE?
NO. WHY ARE YOU DRESSED THAT WAY, BATGIRL?

JEEZ, DOESN'T THIS GETUP FOOL ANYBODY?
WE, *uh*... WE'RE TRYING TO CHEER ROBIN UP.
IS THERE SOMETHING WRONG?

WELL, HE'S BEEN FEELING LIKE ALL WE DO IS FIGHT KILLERS AND PSYCHOS.
SO WE THOUGHT SOME EASILY-BEATEN LIGHTWEIGHTS MIGHT HELP.
I SEE. I'D BE SURPRISED IF THERE WASN'T MORE TO IT THAN THAT.

IF YOU CONTINUE IN YOUR ATTEMPT, MAKE VERY SURE NO ONE IS ENDANGERED.
AND BATGIRL, NEXT TIME YOU GO UNDERCOVER, CHANGE THE WAY YOU MOVE--
--YOU MAY DRESS DIFFERENTLY BUT YOU STILL MOVE LIKE A SUPERHERO.

SO NIGHTWING DECIDED TO CALL IT A NIGHT?
YEAH, SO I ASKED HIM TO TAKE MY OUTFIT BACK WITH HIM.
SUCH A PROMISING CAREER, CUT DOWN IN ITS PRIME.
HO HO.
HEY... WHAT'S THAT?
Gotham
Federal Bank
WHAT'S WHAT?
Oh, YOU MEAN THAT PERSON DRESSED UP LIKE A LION?
THAT'S NIGHTWING, DRESSED UP LIKE A LION.
I SUPPOSE IT WOULD BE RUDE NOT TO STOP BY.

WHAT THE--?
BATGIRL AND ROBIN? HOW DID YOU FIND ME SO QUICKLY? I MUST--
DON'T BOTHER, NIGHTWING. HE KNOWS.
YOU GOTTA BE KIDDING ME. THERE'S NO WAY HE COULD HAVE SEEN THROUGH THIS THING.
LOOK, GOTHAM'S *WEIRD,* BUT COME *ON.* A LION? WERE YOU GOING TO HOOK UP WITH SCARECROW AND METALLO FOR A WIZARD OF OZ REUNION?
NEVER OCCURRED TO ME...
LISTEN, YOU GUYS, I DO APPRECIATE WHAT YOU'RE TRYING TO DO, BUT I GUESS IT'S MORE THAN JUST THE LUNATICS WE DEAL WITH.
IT JUST FEELS SOMETIMES LIKE IT'S ALL IMMEDIATE STUFF AND--
ATTENTION ALL UNITS. BREAK-IN IN PROGRESS AT THE CORNER OF MORSE AND TUCKER.
--WE NEVER REALLY GET TO ACCOMPLISH ANYTHING PERMANENT.

AAAAAAAH!
HERE'S YOUR COSTUMED VILLAIN, ROBIN.
THIS GUY IS *NOT* WHAT I HAD IN MIND.
SHALL WE DO OUR SUPERHERO THING?
WE SHALL.

WELL, THAT WASN'T TOO BAD.
YEAH, THAT LOOKED EASY COMPARED TO DEALING WITH *THEM*.

Hm?

THIS NUTJOB'S GOT A *GANG*?
WEARING HUBCAPS. ROBIN'S RIGHT, THIS CITY *IS* INSANE.

THAT WAS INVIGORATING.
YEAH. LISTEN, THE COPS'LL BE HERE SOON. I THINK I'M GOING TO CALL IT A NIGHT.

COME ON, NIGHTWING. ENOUGH IS ENOUGH. THERE'S RIDICULOUS AND THEN THERE'S--
FLOWERS

YAAAAA!

oh NO oh NO oh NO oh NO THIS CAN'T BE HAPPENING PLEASE.
UM... O-KAY.
HI. I'M ROBIN. WANT TO TELL ME WHY YOU'RE DRESSED UP LIKE THAT?

PLEASE PLEASE PLEASE DON'T TELL MY DAD. HE ALREADY THINKS I'M THE WORLD'S BIGGEST IMBECILE.
I CAN JUST HEAR HIM NOW-- "YOU'RE AN IMBECILE FOR DOING IT IN THE FIRST PLACE, PHIL, AND YOU'RE A BIGGER IMBECILE FOR GETTING CAUGHT. WHY DID--"
SO YOUR NAME'S PHIL?

WHAT? WHAT? NO! NO, IT'S... IT'S...
UM... WELL... CHLOROPHIL.

CHLOROPHYLL. RIGHT.
NO, NO-- ACTUALLY, IT'S CHLORO*PHIL*. SEE, IT'S A LITTLE PUN ON MY NAME AND THE FACT THAT I SPECIALIZE IN ROBBING, Y'KNOW... NURSERIES.

SCOTT'S FLOWERS
WHY?
WELL, BECAUSE, Y'KNOW, CHLOROPHYLL IS INTEGRAL TO THE PHOTOSYNTHESIS PROCESS. IT--
I *KNOW* WHAT CHLOROPHYLL IS. WHY DO YOU KNOCK OVER PLANT STORES?
BECAUSE... BECAUSE, Y'KNOW... I'M AN IMBECILE.

SEE, CINDI SAID SHE WOULDN'T GO OUT WITH ME BECAUSE I DON'T HAVE THE NERVE TO DO ANYTHING DARING LIKE GREG SO I THOUGHT I'D PROVE HER WRONG.
BY RIPPING OFF A *FLOWER* SHOP. GOT SOME I.D., CHLORO?

YEAH. THIS WAS MY FIRST TIME, I SWEAR...
... AND I COULDN'T EVEN FIGURE OUT HOW TO, Y'KNOW, PICK THE LOCK. THE WHOLE IDEA'S KINDA IMBECILIC, *huh*?
WELL, IT'S NOT THE BRIGHTEST THING I'VE EVER HEARD... BUT I'VE HEARD A LOT DUMBER.

AND SPEAK OF THE DEVIL...
WOW, AM I OUTCLASSED.
WHATCHA GOT, ROBIN?

THIS IS PHIL NATTERLY, A.K.A. CHLOROPHIL--
--WHO THE BATCOMPUTER SAYS IS A HIGH SCHOOL SENIOR, BOTANY CLUB PRESIDENT AND ALL-AROUND GOOD KID MAKING A REALLY BAD MISTAKE.

AND WHO I'M PRETTY SURE HAS LEARNED SOMETHING TONIGHT AND ISN'T GOING TO BE MAKING THE SAME MISTAKE AGAIN. AM I RIGHT, PHIL?

oh...oh, YOU BET! YOU BET!
I DON'T CARE WHAT CINDI SAYS! NO MORE LIFE OF CRIME FOR ME! I MAY BE AN IMBECILE, Y'KNOW, BUT I'M NOT STUPID!

AND SO YOU LET HIM GO?
YEAH. HE'S GRADUATING NEXT YEAR, AND HE REALLY HADN'T DONE ANYTHING WRONG YET. AND I'M PRETTY SURE HE'S NOT GOING TO.

YOU SEEM TO BE IN A BETTER MOOD.
I AM. I FEEL LIKE I DID SOME GOOD TONIGHT.
THAT KID MIGHT HAVE REALLY GOTTEN INTO SOME TROUBLE HE WOULDN'T HAVE BEEN ABLE TO GET OUT OF, AND SCREWED UP HIS WHOLE LIFE.

YOU KNOW, YOU DID SOME OTHER PRETTY IMPRESSIVE THINGS, TOO. NOT EVERYONE TAKES DOWN A GUN-WIELDING MANIAC SINGLE-HANDED.
BEING A GUIDANCE COUNSELOR'S A GREAT THING, BUT DOES IT HAVE QUITE THE SAME RUSH?

YEAH, I GUESS IT'S NICE TO HAVE A MIX, *huh*?
ANYHOW, I'M BEAT. I'LL SEE YOU GUYS TOMORROW.
oh, AND DICK? BABS?
THANKS FOR... FOR CARING.

BOY, HE'S A GOOD KID.
INDEED HE IS. I AM MOST GRATIFIED TO SEE THAT HIS SPIRITS ARE ONCE AGAIN BUOYANT.
THANK YOU FOR YOUR ASSISTANCE, ALFRED.
IT WAS MY PLEASURE, SIR.
ASSISTANCE? WHAT ASSIST--
WAIT A MINUTE...
NO. *NO*. THERE IS NO WAY... ARE YOU TELLING ME--
I ADMIT NOTHING. AFTER ALL...
I MAY BE MERELY A BUTLER, BUT I'M NOT... Y'KNOW ... AN IMBECILE.
THE END!

CHAPTER 3: SIX HOURS TO KILL

ROBIN

ROBIN

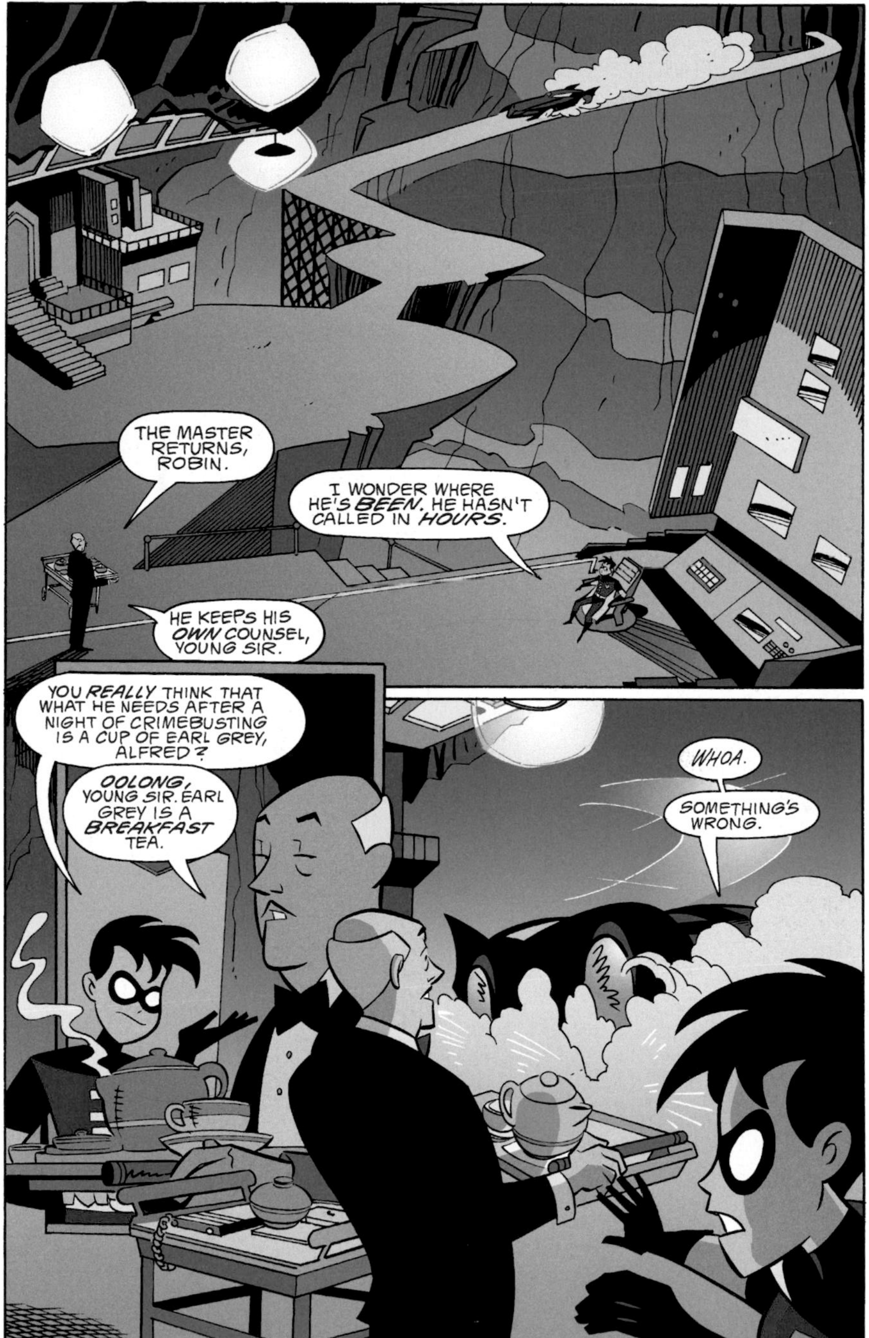
THE MASTER RETURNS, ROBIN.
I WONDER WHERE HE'S BEEN. HE HASN'T CALLED IN HOURS.
HE KEEPS HIS OWN COUNSEL, YOUNG SIR.
YOU REALLY THINK THAT WHAT HE NEEDS AFTER A NIGHT OF CRIMEBUSTING IS A CUP OF EARL GREY, ALFRED?
OOLONG, YOUNG SIR. EARL GREY IS A BREAKFAST TEA.
WHOA.
SOMETHING'S WRONG.

SIX HOURS TO KILL
DOWN, ALFRED!
CHUCK DIXON-writer • JOE STATON-penciller
TERRY BEATTY-inker • LEE LOUGHRIDGE- colorist
TIM HARKINS-letterer • FRANK BERRIOS-asst. ed.
BOB SCHRECK-editor • BATMAN created by BOB KANE

BATMAN!
ROBIN... ALFRED...

... POISONED... DEADLY... NOT MUCH TIME...
Unhh...

WHO DID THIS?
HOW WERE YOU POISONED, SIR?
... SIX HOURS TO LIVE...

uhhhhhh...

WHAT *NOW?*

I'M NOT *CERTAIN.*

NO RECORD OF AN OZZIE FISH IN OUR CRIMINAL FILES.
TANKS? WHAT KIND OF TANKS?
WHAT CASE WAS HE WORKING ON, ALFRED?
HE WAS ATTEMPTING TO DISCOVER THE WHEREABOUTS OF THE SWAG FROM THE TEMPLETON DIAMOND HEIST.
THAT'S "GOGGLES" McCRACKEN'S GANG.
THEY'RE STRICTLY SMASH AND GRAB TYPES.
THEY WOULD HAVE JUST SHOT BATMAN.
CAN WE FORESTALL THE SLEUTHING UNTIL MASTER BRUCE IS MOVED?
IT IS URGENT WE GET HIM ON OXYGEN.
COMING!

uh... WOULDN'T IT BE BETTER... uh... IF HE WAS IN A HOSPITAL?
WE WOULD BE UNABLE TO SATISFACTORILY EXPLAIN HIS CONDITION.
THIS WOULD DELAY ANY CARE HE WOULD RECEIVE.

AND, AS HE SAID, HE ONLY HAS SIX HOURS.
LESS THAN THAT, ALFRED. WE DON'T KNOW WHEN HE WAS POISONED.
AN EXCELLENT POINT.

I WILL DRAW SOME BLOOD.
YOU'LL NEED A SAMPLE TO AID IN YOUR INVESTIGATION.

MY INVESTIGATION?
WHAT AM I SUPPOSED TO DO WITH THAT?

WE ALREADY KNOW OF AN EXPERT TOXICOLOGIST.
IT WILL BE UP TO YOU TO FIND HER. AND THERE'S VERY LITTLE TIME.

NOT BAD. NOT BAD AT ALL.
the ICEBERG LOUNGE
THIS PLACE IS HOPPIN', PENGUIN.
I SHOULD HAVE DONE THIS YEARS AGO, BOYS.
I'VE MADE SO MUCH MORE FILTHY CASH SINCE BECOMING A "LEGITIMATE" BUSINESSMAN.
I THINK I LIKED YOU BETTER AS A CROOK, PENGIE.
THE BAT'S BRAT.
- WHAT ARE YOU DOING HERE ALONE?
WHO SAYS I'M ALONE?
oh...

uhhh... LET'S HEAR WHAT THE SQUIRT HAS TO SAY, GENTLEMEN.
WE'RE NOT HERE FOR YOU, COBBLEPOT.
WE'RE LOOKING FOR POISON IVY.
I'M A PENGUIN, NOT A STOOL PIGEON.
YOU'D GIVE UP YOUR OWN MOTHER.
I WASN'T GOING TO JAIL FOR THAT WITCH.
LOOK, IVY AND THAT QUINN CREATURE WERE IN HERE LAST NIGHT.
BUT THEY DON'T REALLY CONFIDE IN ME.
HOW MUCH OF THIS STACK ARE YOU REPORTING FOR TAXES?
VERY WELL...

GOTHAM BOTANICAL GARDENS
KLIK
OH, MAN...
KLIK
POO.
KLIK
IK.
KLIK
UGH.
CLOSED

ENTRANCE
Y'KNOW THE *WORST* PART OF BEIN' ON THE LAM?
NO, I *DON'T* KNOW, HARL.

NO *CABLE*. JUST TEN CHANNELS.
THERE'S *NOTHIN'* ON THIS LATE.
YOU SAY THE SAME THING WHEN THERE'RE TWO *HUNDRED* CHANNELS.
I'M *BOOOORED*. CAN'T WE DO SOME *CRIMES* AND JUNK?
APPARENTLY YOU DON'T UNDERSTAND WHAT "IN HIDING" *MEANS*, HARLEY.

YOU REALLY TALK TO THEM PLANTS, IVES?
AND THEY UNDERSTAND EVERY WORD. DON'T 'OO, 'OO LI'L DARLIN'?
LET ME TRY.
GROW! GROW FASTER, YA STUPID WEED!!
I SWEAR, YOU TRY MY PATIENCE, YOU LITTLE...
eep!
DON'T MEAN TO BREAK UP THIS SPECIAL MOMENT...
...BUT I NEED YOUR HELP.
THE BOY HOSTAGE!

YOU NEED OUR "HELP"? WHAT KIND OF TRICK IS THIS?
DON'T TALK. JUST FIGHT.
NO TRICKS.
YEAH... RIGHT.
BOOM BOOM
BOOM
BOOM
BOOM
OOP!
YOU IMBECILE, THE PLANTS!
BOOM BOOM BOOM
WHAT? THEY'LL GROW BACK!

BATMAN'S BEEN POISONED. WE-- I CAN'T IDENTIFY THE TOXIN.
THERE'S NOT MUCH TIME. YOU'RE MY ONLY HOPE, IVY.
LIKE I CARE? LET HIM DIE.
BATSY'S... DYING?
IVY, I JUST HATE THE IDEA OF HIM DYING LIKE THAT. SICK, IN PAIN.
GOOD RIDDANCE. HE'S JUST A THORN IN OUR SIDE.
I CAN'T STAND THE IDEA OF HIM DYING, ALL ALONE...
...WHERE WE CAN'T SEE IT.
THAT WOULD BE A TRAGEDY.

IF IT'S A RECOGNIZED TOXIN, I SHOULD BE ABLE TO SEPARATE IT FROM THE BLOOD.
AND IDENTIFY IT.
YOU SAID HE HAS A FEVER?
AND CONVULSIONS, AND DIFFICULTY BREATHING.
IT'S A NEUROTOXIN. AND I DON'T HAVE AN ANTIDOTE FOR IT.
WHAT KIND OF TOXIN?
IT'S NOT PLANT. IT'S ANIMAL.
YOU'LL NEED THE ANTITOXIN, IF THERE IS ONE.
WITHOUT IT, NO TREATMENT WILL WORK. HIS HEART WILL STOP.
NO...
POOR KID.
WELL, LOOK AT THE BRIGHT SIDE.
YOU'LL GET ALL HIS STUFF.

IT'S SOME KIND OF ANIMAL, ALFRED.
NO CLUE AS TO ITS GENUS OR SPECIES?
IT COULD BE A SNAKE OR A SPIDER OR...

I BANDAGED SOME PECULIAR MARKS ON THE MASTER'S ARM.
WHAT KIND OF MARKS?
RAISED CIRCLES.

OZZIE... BLUE RING... TANKS... FISH... BLUE RING... TANKS... FISH...
THERE IS A CHANCE HIS MUTTERINGS WERE MEANINGLESS—
BLUE RING... OZZIE... FISH... TANKS.
FISH TANKS!
...

MASTER TIMOTHY?
SIR?

GOTHAM AQUARIUM
NOW WHAT?

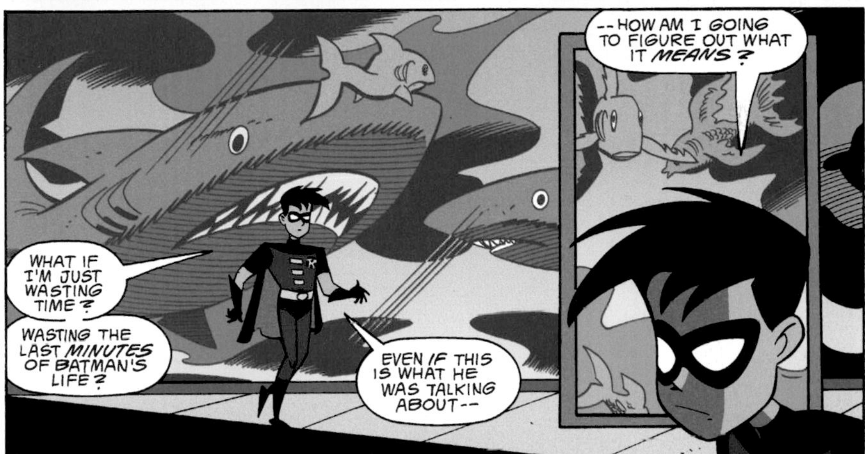
WHAT IF I'M JUST WASTING TIME?
WASTING THE LAST MINUTES OF BATMAN'S LIFE?
EVEN IF THIS IS WHAT HE WAS TALKING ABOUT--
--HOW AM I GOING TO FIGURE OUT WHAT IT MEANS?

Aquatic Life of AUSTRALIA
AND IF I'M WAY OFF, THEN HE DIES.
NO SECOND CHANCES.
Whoa.
NOT OZZIE FISH.
AUSSIE FISH.
N
Australia

BLUE RING, BLUE RING, BLUE RING.
STUDDED STARFISH

BLUE-RINGED OCTOPUS
OCTOPUS, MACULOSA
YEAH...
OUR LITTLE CUP OF POISON.
AND THE TEMPLETON DIAMONDS.

UNNH!

GOGGLES McCRACKEN...
I'M NOT SURPRISED. THE BAT WAS HERE EARLIER AND NOW HIS LITTLE PAL.

HE WASN'T EXPECTING US TO BE HERE AS SECURITY GUARDS, EITHER.
HE FOUND OUR DIAMOND STASH, TOO.
henh.
BUT THE OCTOPUS IS QUICKER THAN THE EYE.
AND I WASN'T ABOUT TO WASTE THE ANTIVENOM ON HIM.

TELL ME WHERE THE ANTIDOTE IS.
BATMAN IS DYING, GOGGLES. YOU DON'T WANT THAT ON YOUR CONSCIENCE.
DON'T BOTHER ME, KID.
I'LL EVEN MAKE IT A TWO-FER!

uh?
GET HIM!
WHUZZAT?
unnh!
UNGH!
LITTLE...
WOO?
OUCH.
I'M GONNA CRUSH YOU!
uh oh.

YOU COULD MAKE THIS EASIER ON YOURSELF AND GIVE ME THE ANTIDOTE.
NO WAY, BRAT!
SNAP!
huh?
WHERE ARE YOU? WHERE'D YOU GO?
FIRST, TELL ME WHERE THE ANTIDOTE IS.
AND SAVE THE BAT'S LIFE?
WHAT DO I LOOK LIKE TO YOU? A CHUMP?

YOU CAN'T GET AWAY FROM *ME*.
I GOT YOU RIGHT WHERE I --
blubb!
BLUE-RINGED OCTOPUS
KRIIISSH!

AAAAAAH!
GET IT OFFA ME! GET IT OFFA ME!

DONT HAVE A COW.
WHAT A BIG BABY.
OOH! OOH! OW!

I'M GONNA DIE! I'M GONNA DIE!
YOU DON'T HAVE TO, GOGGLES.

YOU CAN TELL ME WHERE THE ANTITOXIN IS.
BECAUSE YOU'RE SURE NOT GONNA FIND IT ON YOUR OWN.

oh--OKAY.

QUITE A NIGHT OUT FOR YOU, ROBIN.

YOU FOUND THE TEMPLETON DIAMONDS. BROUGHT BACK THE ANTITOXIN. ROUNDED UP THE McCRACKEN GANG.
AND SAVED MY LIFE.

ALL IN A NIGHT'S WORK.
PLUS A COUPLE OF OTHER DIVIDENDS.

WHAT'RE YOU LOOKING AT?
ACTUALLY, I'M NOT SURE.
CAUTION: BIOHAZARD RISK
THE END

CHAPTER 4: TUESDAY NIGHT

ROBIN

ROBIN

CO.
1902

KA-BOOO
TUESDAY NIGHT
SCOTT PETERSON - WRITER * CRAIG ROUSSEAU - GUEST PENCILLER
DAN DAVIS - GUEST INKER * LEE LOUGHRIDGE - COLORIST * ALBERT T. DEGUZMAN - LETTERER
HARVEY RICHARDS - ASSISTANT EDITOR * JOAN HILTY - FIRE CHIEF
BATMAN Created by BOB KANE

WELL?
NO ONE UP THERE.
THE LOWER FLOORS ARE ALL SECURED?
THE FIREFIGHTERS HAD ALREADY GOTTEN ALL OF THEM EXCEPT THE TOP.
THIS IS THE THIRD BIG BLAZE TONIGHT. THINK IT'S A PATTERN?
THREE ISN'T THAT UNUSUAL. WHO'S SHE?
THAT'S THE OWNER OF THE BUILDING-- *SUZANNE CORMIER.*
G C F D
WANT ME TO CHECK HER OUT?
THIS PLACE WENT UP MUCH FASTER THAN IT SHOULD HAVE.
YES, CHECK HER OUT.

WELL, ALFRED SAYS CORMIER OWNS ABOUT TWO DOZEN BUILDINGS THROUGHOUT GOTHAM AND SEEMS TO BE CLEAN...
WHAT TOOK SO LONG TO FIND THAT OUT?
OH, YEAH, SORRY ABOUT THAT. ALFRED AND I GOT DISCONNECTED AND THEN THE BATCOMPUTER WAS ACTING A LITTLE SLUGGISH.
HAVE ALFRED CHECK YOUR RADIO AS SOON AS YOU GET BACK TONIGHT.
YOU GOT IT. HEY, ANY CHANCE--
...
WAIT.
THERE'S *ANOTHER* ONE...
...AND THIS TIME THERE ARE PEOPLE TRAPPED IN THERE.

THE TUB WAS A SMART MOVE.
ONE.

TWO.
HERE.
RRRRUMBLE
WE MIGHT BE ABLE TO--
CEILING'S GONE.
GO.

ISN'T THAT SUZANNE CORMIER?
THE WOMAN WHO OWNED THE OTHER BUILDING?
THIS PLACE WASN'T ONE OF HERS.
BATMAN!
WHAT ARE YOU DOING HERE?
WELL, I--I HEARD ABOUT THE FIRE AND SO I--
YOU DON'T OWN THIS BUILDING.
NOT EXACTLY. I BOUGHT IT, BUT IT'S IN MY SON'S NAME.
RESTA
WAIT A MINUTE... YOU THINK THAT I HAD SOMETHING TO DO WITH THIS?
YOU ARE MORE THAN WELCOME TO LOOK THROUGH ALL MY RECORDS, BATMAN.
IF THERE'S ANY CONNECTION BETWEEN ME AND THESE FIRES, I HOPE YOU CAN FIND IT.
THOSE CHILDREN YOU SAVED?

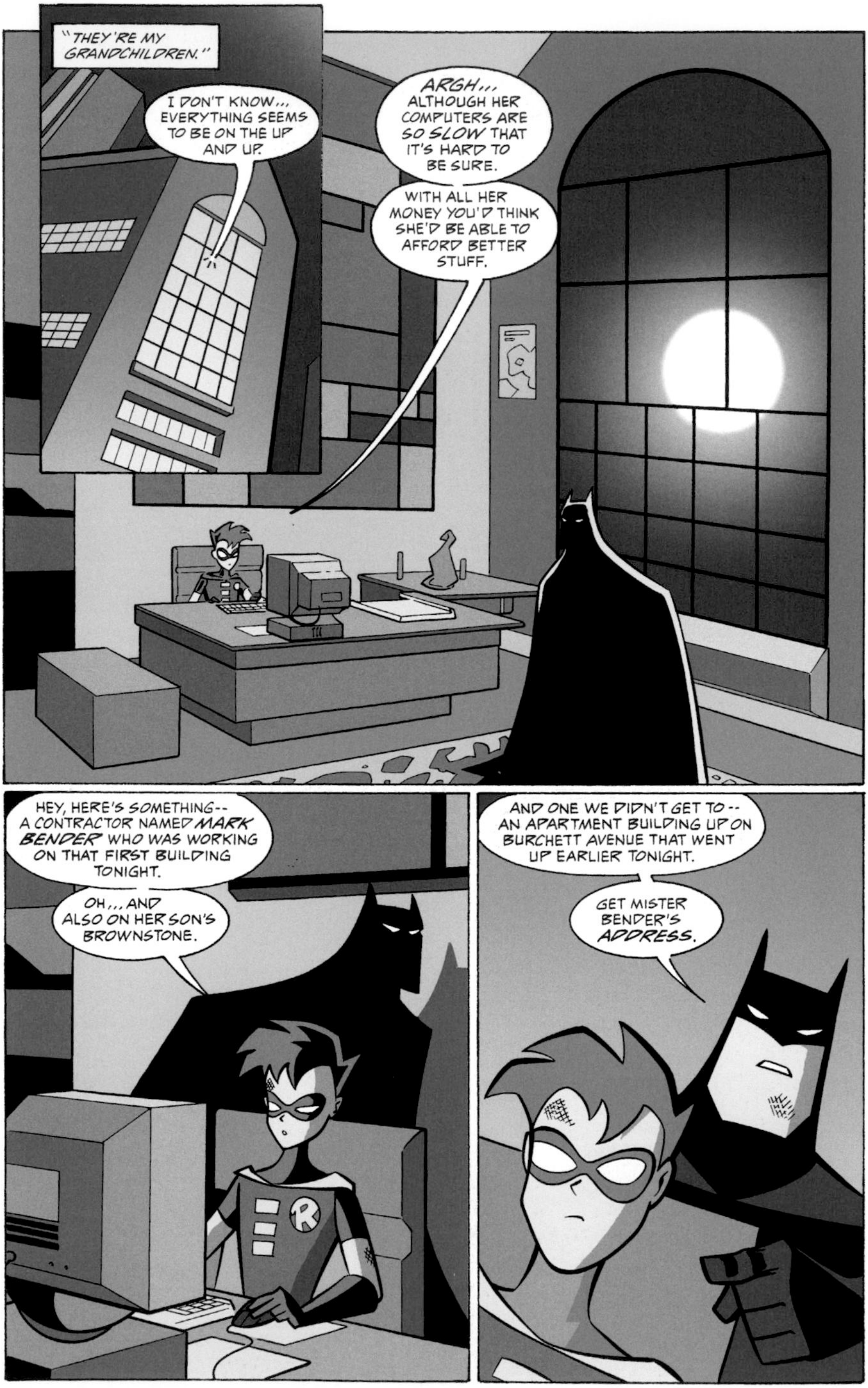

"THEY'RE MY GRANDCHILDREN."
I DON'T KNOW... EVERYTHING SEEMS TO BE ON THE UP AND UP.
ARGH... ALTHOUGH HER COMPUTERS ARE SO SLOW THAT IT'S HARD TO BE SURE.
WITH ALL HER MONEY YOU'D THINK SHE'D BE ABLE TO AFFORD BETTER STUFF.

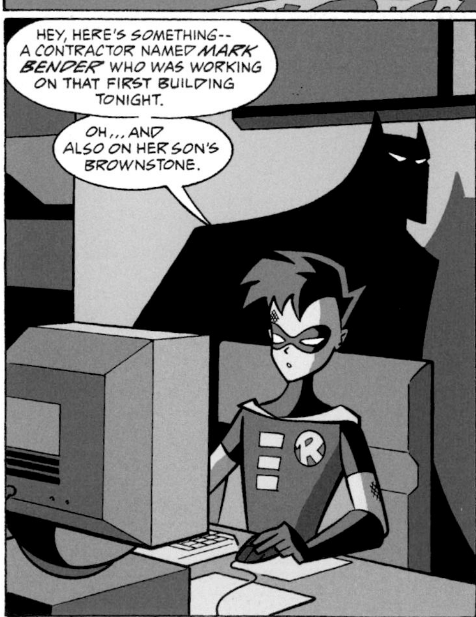
HEY, HERE'S SOMETHING-- A CONTRACTOR NAMED MARK BENDER WHO WAS WORKING ON THAT FIRST BUILDING TONIGHT.
OH... AND ALSO ON HER SON'S BROWNSTONE.

AND ONE WE DIDN'T GET TO -- AN APARTMENT BUILDING UP ON BURCHETT AVENUE THAT WENT UP EARLIER TONIGHT.
GET MISTER BENDER'S ADDRESS.

YAARGH!
LITTLE JUMPY, MISTER BENDER?
GUESS I'M NOT USED TO A COUPLE OF GUYS IN MASKS WAKING ME UP IN THE MIDDLE OF THE NIGHT!
DECIDED NOT TO STAY UP AND SEE THE FRUITS OF YOUR HARD WORK?
WHAT ARE YOU TALKING ABOUT?
THREE OF THE BUILDINGS YOU'VE WORKED ON WENT UP IN FLAMES TONIGHT. YOU DON'T SEEM CONCERNED.
HEY, I GET UP AT FIVE IN THE MORNING, SO I GO TO BED EARLY. I DIDN'T EVEN HEAR ABOUT ANY OF THIS.
WHICH BUILDINGS?
THE ONES OWNED BY SUZANNE CORMIER.
BUT WHICH ONES? I'VE WORKED ON DOZENS OF 'EM.

I HANDLE ALL HER HEATING AND COOLING SYSTEMS. I'M CURRENTLY INSTALLING TOP-OF-THE-LINE SYSTEMS ON A LOT OF HER UNITS.
INCLUDING *THESE?*
YEAH, I'VE DONE ALL THESE RECENTLY.
BUT LISTEN, THERE'S NO WAY IT *COULD* BE THE SYSTEMS-- THEY'RE ALL THE VERY LATEST, POWERED BY THE *XJ9*, LINKED TO A MAINFRAME IN--
THEY'RE COMPUTER-OPERATED? THAT EXPLAINS IT.
IT'S THE SUNSPOTS.
WHAT? YOU'RE SAYING THAT SOMETHING A COUPLE MILLION MILES AWAY--
NINETY-THREE MILLION. SERIOUSLY, *BATMAN?* YOU REALLY THINK THAT'S IT?
THE STORMS ON THE SURFACE OF THE SUN ARE SEVENTEEN TIMES THE SIZE OF THE EARTH. THE SUN HAS JUST ROTATED ENOUGH FOR THEM TO BE FACING OUR DIRECTION.
THE *ELECTROMAGNETIC WAVES* THEY CREATE ARE ENORMOUSLY POWERFUL. THAT'S WHAT WAS INTERFERING WITH YOUR RADIO AND CORMIER'S COMPUTERS EARLIER.
IF THE SIGNALS COMING FROM THE MAINFRAME GOT *SCRAMBLED*...
THEY COULD CAUSE THE SYSTEM TO *OVERHEAT*.

"LISTEN, THERE'S ANOTHER BUILDING, A HIGH-RISE ON PAROBECK AVENUE."
FINALLY GOT THROUGH TO ALFRED. SEEMS WE'VE GOT GOOD NEWS AND BAD NEWS.
THE GOOD NEWS IS THAT THE SUB-BASEMENT CAN BE COMPLETELY SELF-CONTAINED--AND IT'S WHERE THE FIRE STARTED.
SO, ISOLATE THE FIRE AND IT'LL BE EASIER TO GET IT UNDER CONTROL.
WELL... THE BAD NEWS IS THAT IN THEIR PANIC, THE WORKERS RAN OFF AND LEFT THE ISOLATING DOOR OPEN.
AND THEY THINK THERE'S SOMEONE TRAPPED ON ONE OF THE TOP FLOORS.

IS HE--?

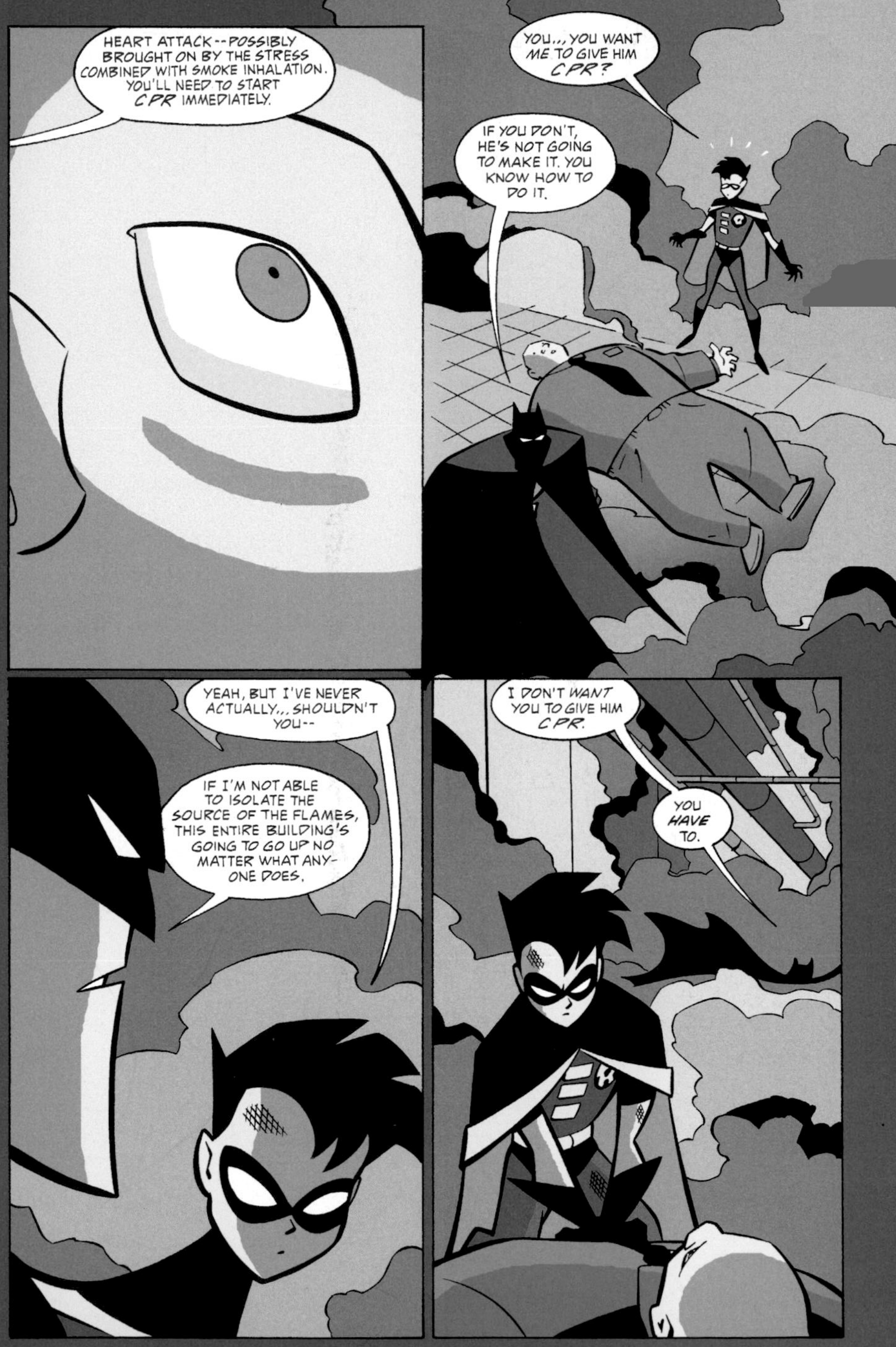
HEART ATTACK--POSSIBLY BROUGHT ON BY THE STRESS COMBINED WITH SMOKE INHALATION. YOU'LL NEED TO START CPR IMMEDIATELY.
YOU..., YOU WANT ME TO GIVE HIM CPR?
IF YOU DON'T, HE'S NOT GOING TO MAKE IT. YOU KNOW HOW TO DO IT.
YEAH, BUT I'VE NEVER ACTUALLY..., SHOULDN'T YOU--
IF I'M NOT ABLE TO ISOLATE THE SOURCE OF THE FLAMES, THIS ENTIRE BUILDING'S GOING TO GO UP NO MATTER WHAT ANY-ONE DOES.
I DON'T WANT YOU TO GIVE HIM CPR.
YOU HAVE TO.

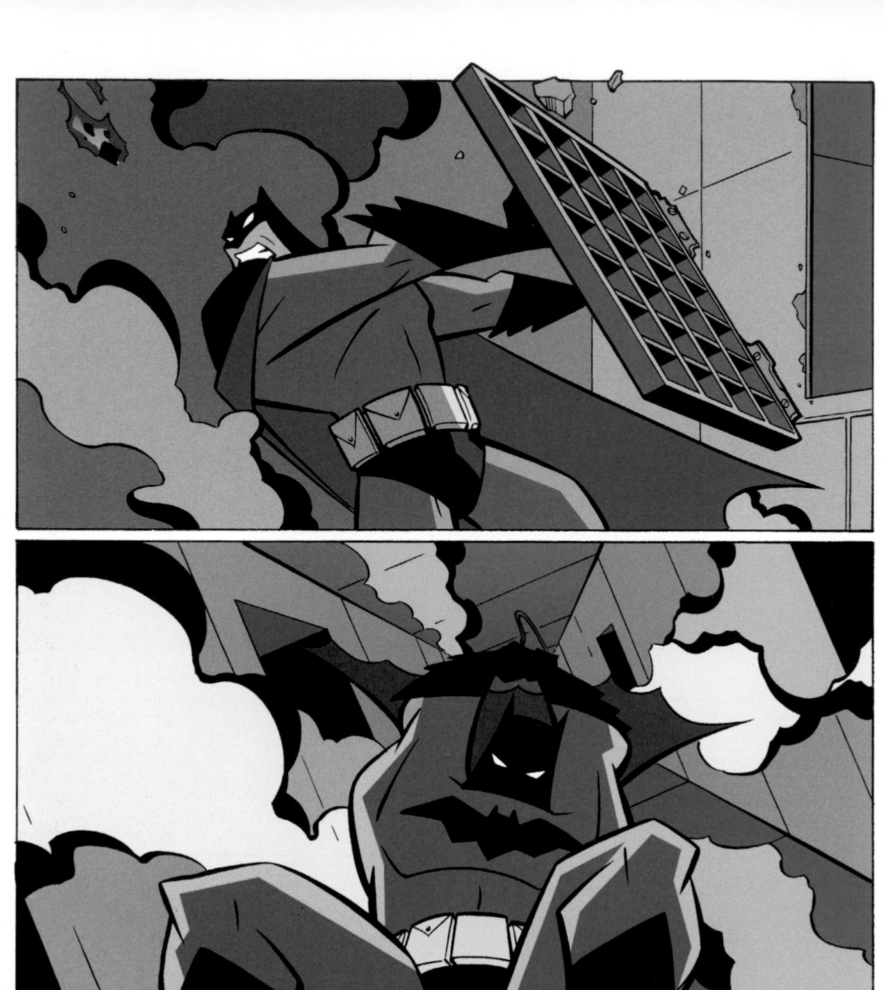

CHAMBER
SECURE

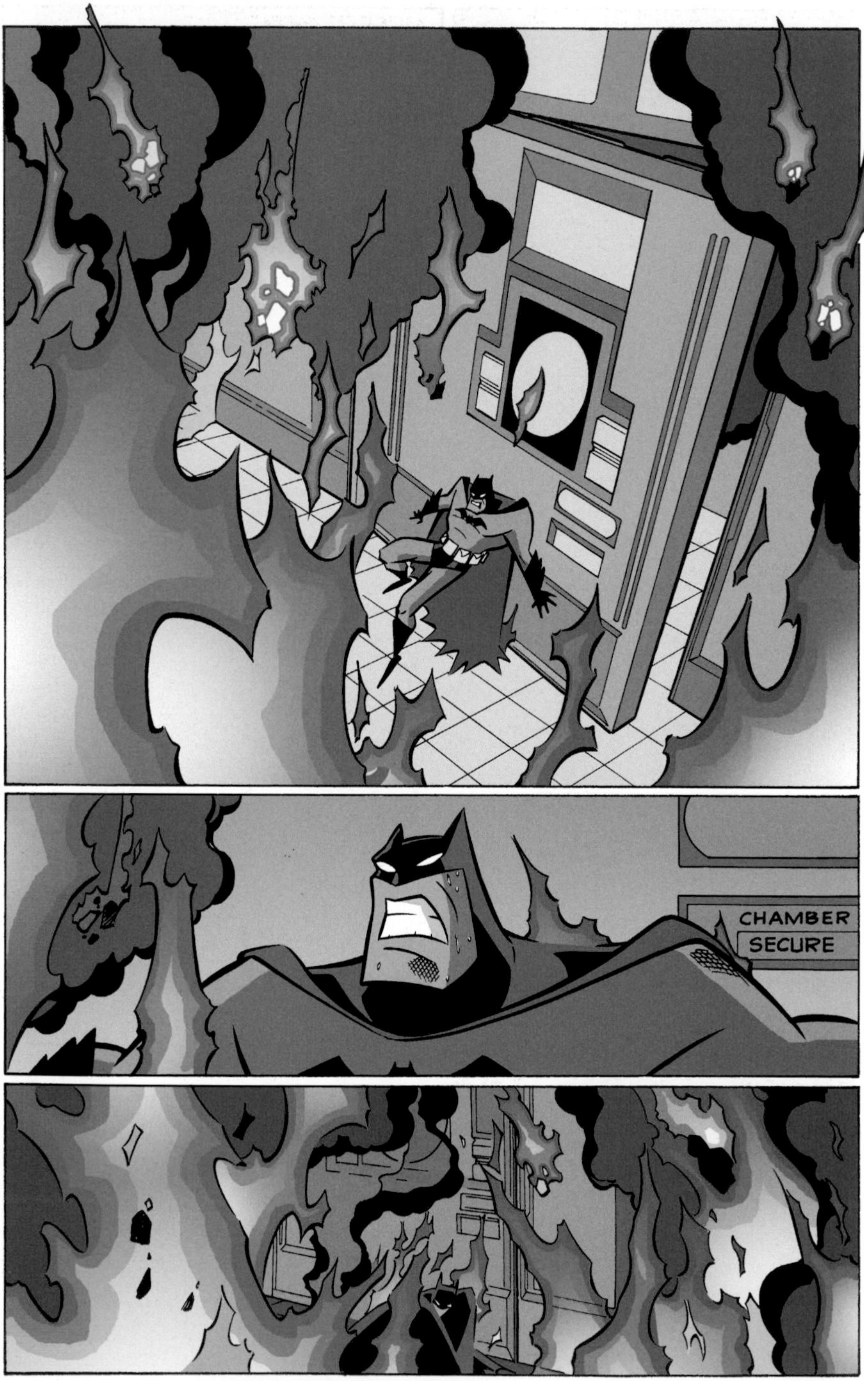

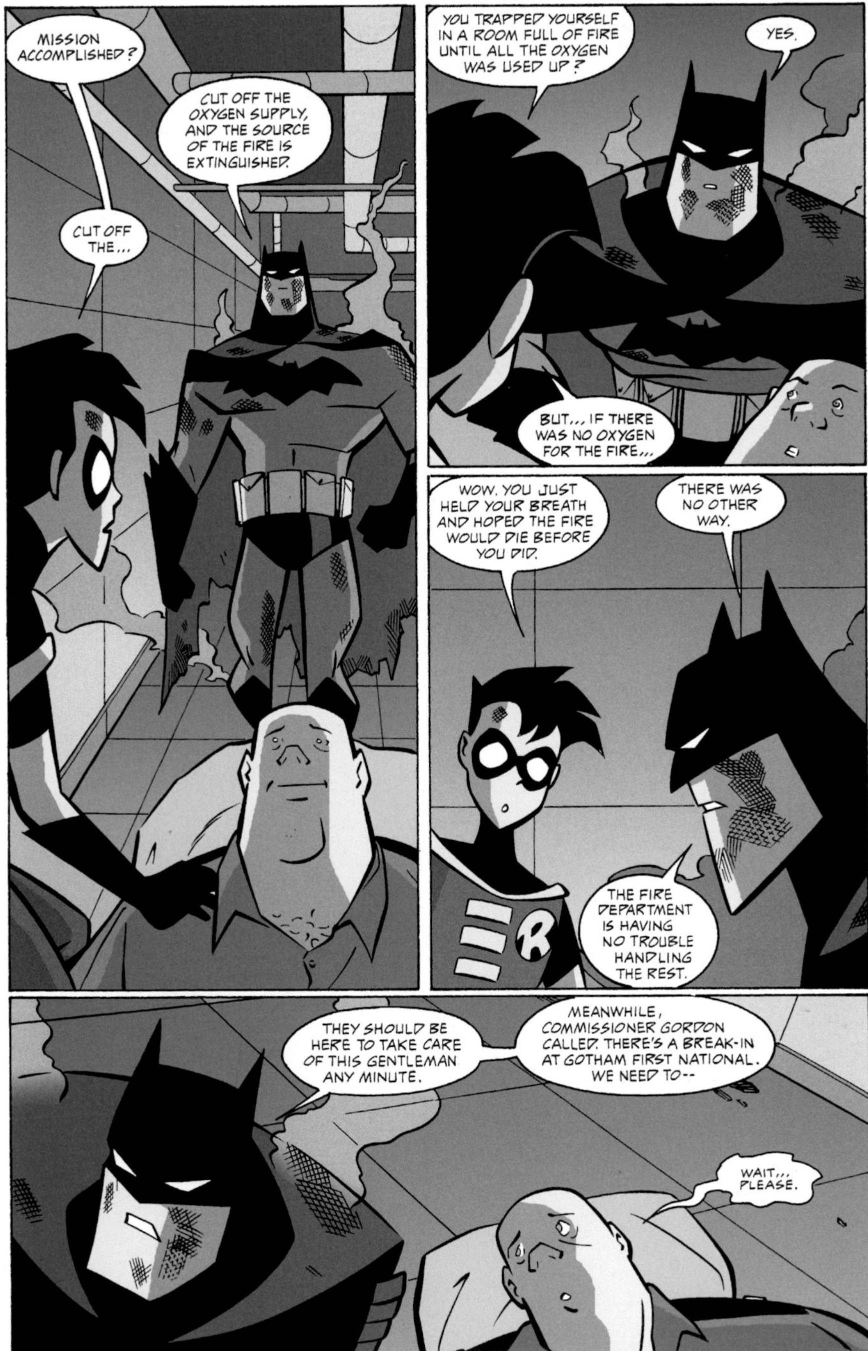
MISSION ACCOMPLISHED?
CUT OFF THE OXYGEN SUPPLY, AND THE SOURCE OF THE FIRE IS EXTINGUISHED.
CUT OFF THE...
YOU TRAPPED YOURSELF IN A ROOM FULL OF FIRE UNTIL ALL THE OXYGEN WAS USED UP?
YES.
BUT... IF THERE WAS NO OXYGEN FOR THE FIRE...
WOW. YOU JUST HELD YOUR BREATH AND HOPED THE FIRE WOULD DIE BEFORE YOU DID.
THERE WAS NO OTHER WAY.
THE FIRE DEPARTMENT IS HAVING NO TROUBLE HANDLING THE REST.
THEY SHOULD BE HERE TO TAKE CARE OF THIS GENTLEMAN ANY MINUTE.
MEANWHILE, COMMISSIONER GORDON CALLED. THERE'S A BREAK-IN AT GOTHAM FIRST NATIONAL. WE NEED TO--
WAIT... PLEASE.

TH-THANK... YOU.
NO PROBLEM AT ALL.
SHEESH. SOME NIGHT, HUH?
YOU GUYS GOT A NAME FOR NIGHTS LIKE THIS?
YES.
EMS
TUESDAY.
END

CHAPTER 5: MASTERWORK

ROBIN

SCOTT PETERSON
master writer
TIM LEVINS
master penciller
TERRY BEATTY
master inker
LEE LOUGHRIDGE
master colorist
ALBERT T. DE GUZMAN
master letterer
HARVEY RICHARDS
assistant master
JOAN HILTY
master editor
Batman created by
Bob Kane

He stands, high above his city. It has all led to this one moment.]

He breathes deeply, filling his lungs with the oxygen necessary to fulfill his task.]
But there is more to the act than]
than simple physical need.]

As he breathes in the scent of his city, tasting its unique odor, imbibing its aroma, he becomes.]
He becomes one with the city.]
He becomes Gotham.]

It holds no secrets from him.]
He knows all it knows.]
Its needs, its desires, its]
!its needs, its desires, its every little wish.]
And he knows that he is]
he is the answer to it all.]

NO! THAT'S NOT... THAT'S NOT GOOD.
THAT'S STILL MISSING THE ESSENCE, THE POWER, THE DRAMA... THE... THE VERY PATHOS. NEED THE PATHOS TO MAKE IT BIG TIME.
OKAY, HOW ABOUT...

Yes.]
I am ready.]

YES!

"OKAY, LET'S GET HIM TO THE CRIME SCENE, BLAH BLAH BLAH, FIGURE OUT LATER HOW HE GOT THERE..."
Like the world's greatest two-legged bloodhound, he cases the scene, unearthing things other experts would never notice.]

There is nothing, no speck of dust, no hair fiber, no remnant of skin so small it will escape his notice.]

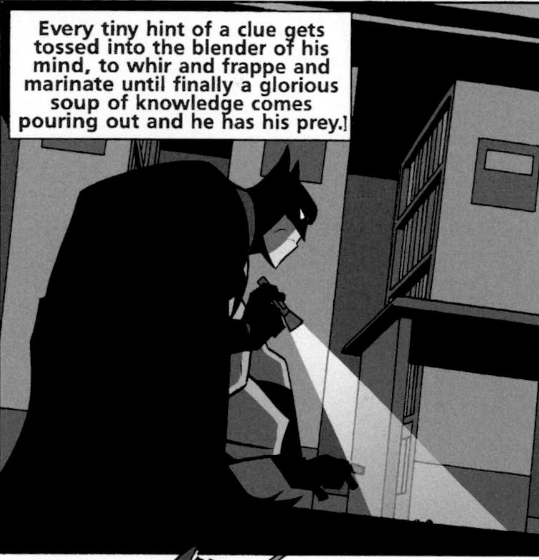
Every tiny hint of a clue gets tossed into the blender of his mind, to whir and frappe and marinate until finally a glorious soup of knowledge comes pouring out and he has his prey.]

He wastes not an ounce of energy, every movement deliberate, thought out well in advance, always prepared.]
He is the bogeyman, the monster under your bed, the walking ghost, everything scary you've ever dared to imagine. He is...]
GOTHAM CENTRAL LIBRARY

"...HE IS... HE IS... WHAT?"
WONDERING WHAT YOU WERE DOING IN THE GOTHAM LIBRARY AFTER CLOSING TIME, MISS STAINES.
YAAAAAAGH!
YOU... HOW... HOW DID YOU *KNOW*?
THERE WERE MINUTE TRACES OF FRESH *KYOTA INK* ON THE FLOOR. SINCE THE FLOOR HAD BEEN CLEANED A FEW HOURS BEFORE, THE INK WAS CLEARLY NEW.
KYOTA IS MADE IN *OSAKA*. ONLY *ONE* STORE IN GOTHAM CARRIES IT.
STORE RECORDS SAID YOU WERE ONE OF SEVEN PEOPLE TO HAVE PURCHASED INK IN THE PAST MONTH,
AND YOU RECOGNIZED MY NAME, SO YOU CAME TO ME *FIRST*!
GOTHAMITE
UP CLOSE
by Mel Staines

YOU LIVED THE CLOSEST.
OH.

BUT NOW YOU KNOW I'M WRITING A STORY ON THE MISSING MANUSCRIPTS FOR THE GOTHAMITE--
--SO YOU WANT TO KNOW EVERYTHING I FIGURED OUT, RIGHT?
IS THERE ANYTHING THAT WOULD INTEREST ME?

WITHOUT QUESTION! FOR INSTANCE, I'VE CONCLUDED THAT THE PERP ALMOST CERTAINLY HAS ISSUES WITH AUTHORITY, MAYBE FROM AN OVERBEARING PARENT.
SAID PERP LIKELY ALSO HAS A COMBINATION OF SUPERIORITY AND INFERIORITY COMPLEXES, MAYHAP STEMMING FROM A CHILDHOOD INCIDENT WHEREIN--

WAIT,,, WHERE ARE YOU GOING?
WRITE YOUR LITTLE STORY, MISS STAINES--
--BUT DO NOT CONTAMINATE A CRIME SCENE AGAIN.

HOLD ON! HOW ABOUT THE FACT THAT THE CRIMINAL IS A MASTER OF ARCANE FIGHTING STYLES!
MAN...

HOW DO YOU KNOW THAT?
IEEE-YAAAAH!

HA-HA! GOTCHA!
Uh-uh. NO WAY. I AIN'T SAYIN'. NOT UNLESS YOU TAKE ME WITH YOU.

FINE.

BUT... BUT...

A rustle, a blur...and he is gone, melting back into the night whence he came.]

His destination, his thoughts unknowable.
THEORIES?
WELL, THE LIBRARY WAS BROKEN INTO AND SOME OLD BOOK WAS STOLEN.
THE ORIGINAL MANUSCRIPT TO "ULYSSES."
RIGHT. BUT THERE WERE ALSO EARLIER THEFTS--
--A SCROLL OF ANCIENT CHINESE POETRY, A GUTENBERG BIBLE AND THE FIRST DRAFT OF "HUCKLEBERRY FINN."
ANYTHING IN COMMON?
HARD TO SAY-- THE VARIOUS LIBRARIES ARE KEEPING QUIET, HOPING THE MANUSCRIPTS TURN UP. OH, AND--
...
AND THERE'S BEEN A BREAK-IN AT THE DUTTON GALLERY.

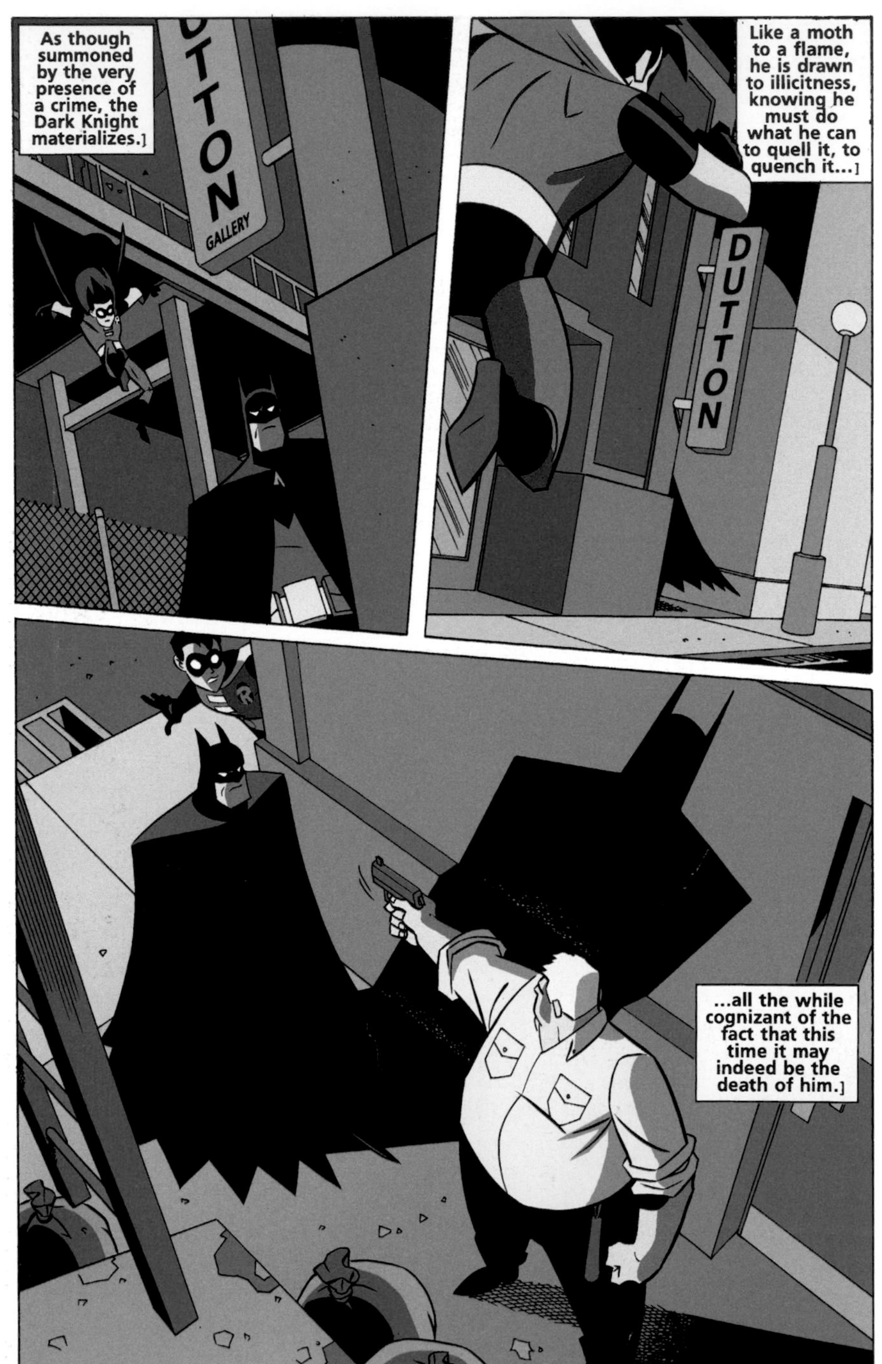

As though summoned by the very presence of a crime, the Dark Knight materializes.]
DUTTON
GALLERY
Like a moth to a flame, he is drawn to illicitness, knowing he must do what he can to quell it, to quench it...]
DUTTON
...all the while cognizant of the fact that this time it may indeed be the death of him.]

A fate eventually inevitable.]
YOU MADE ONE MISTAKE ALREADY.
STOP AT THAT.

For him, perhaps--but never for others.]

Thus has he sworn.]

Whoa... I... I'M SO SORRY... I HAD NO IDEA THAT KID WAS THERE!

I'M SO SORRY.

SMITTY? THAT YOU?

Not all have taken that same oath.

GET YOUR HANDS OFF HIM.

And so the deadly dance begins.

Its tragic, ghastly end is inevitable, surely.]
NO ONE TOUCHES A DUTTON GUARD AND GETS AWAY WITH IT!
A missed clue, turning a half-second too late, overwhelmed by superior numbers...]

There are a million ways for this Dark Knight to meet his maker.

But not this night.

His destiny is delayed once again.

And so the legend continues to grow. With nary a pause--
SO, IF YOU JUST TOOK OUT ALL THE LIBRARY'S GUARDS, WHO'S GONNA BE WATCHING THE LIBRARY'S STUFF?
I'LL ALERT COMMISSIONER GORDON IN A MOMENT. FIRST I WANT A WORD WITH...
--he turns to his next vital object.
...MISS STAINES.
WOW! HOW'D YOU KNOW I WAS IN HERE?
I HEARD THREE PULSES AND COULD TELL TWO OF THEM WERE RATS.
RATS! WHAT?! ARE YOU SERIOUS?!
NO. I HEARD YOU OVERWRITING.
I THOUGHT I WARNED YOU TO STAY AWAY.
FREEDOM OF THE PRESS. I ONLY TAKE ORDERS FROM MY EDITOR, AND I USUALLY IGNORE HIM, TOO.

WELL, YOU MAY HAVE PURCHASED ACCESS TO THE CRIME SCENES FROM THE LIBRARY GUARDS--
--YOU SAID YOU'D PUT THEIR NAMES IN YOUR STORY IN EXCHANGE FOR ADMITTANCE, DIDN'T YOU?--
--BUT ARKHAM'S GUARDS AREN'T SO EASILY BOUGHT.

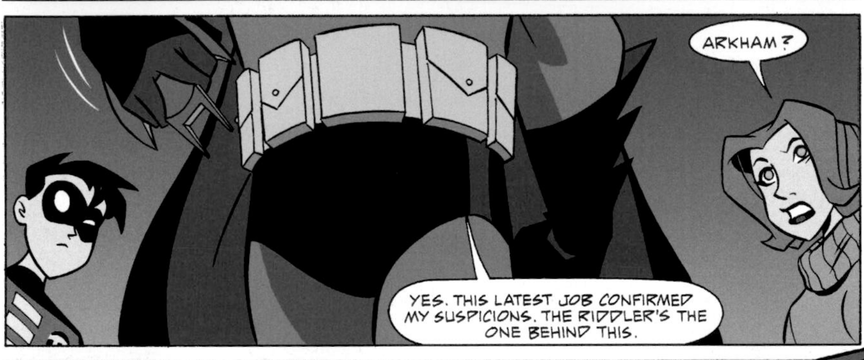
ARKHAM?
YES. THIS LATEST JOB CONFIRMED MY SUSPICIONS. THE RIDDLER'S THE ONE BEHIND THIS.

WHAT?
THE RIDDLER?
YES. HE'S FINALLY CHANGED HIS MODUS OPERANDI. THE SCHEME ITSELF IS SECOND-RATE, BUT AT LEAST HE'S TRYING SOMETHING DIFFERENT.

HE'S NOT SUCCEEDING, OF COURSE. THEY NEVER DO. BUT THEY'RE NEVER SMART ENOUGH TO STOP TRYING.

Suddenly, like a cobra striking sans warning, the tide turns.

Utilizing every skill at her command, she quickly adapts to this new challenge.
M ARCH
LIBR
As always, she is amused how much she can get by simply promising to print someone's name.

Subterfuge, sleight-of-hand, masterful planning...
GOTHAM A
LIBRARY

The Dark Knight will find to his shock and horror he's not the only one capable of lightning-quick reactions.

He'll see--
NEED A HAND WITH THAT?
WHA-?! BUT... BUT YOU WERE--
FOLLOWING YOU THE ENTIRE TIME.
BUT... BUT ARKHAM--
CATCHER IN THE RYE
WAS A RUSE, TO GET YOU TO ACT RECKLESSLY.
IT'S OVER, MISS STAINES.
NO! THIS IS MY STORY! I DECIDE WHEN IT'S OVER!
The look on his face fueled her, granting her precious energy.

He swiftly danced away from her life-taking blade.]
Thoughts pirouetted through his mind like tiny little synaptic ballerinas.]
It all came together, he thought, as the knife cut through the tender dermis of his cape.]
She'd bribed the guards with money and the thought of fame.]
If they'd just let her in, she could write them up in one of her stories.]
They'd be immortal. Or so they believed, and thus believing, they fell.]

They could never confess, lest they lose their gainful employment.
And as they fell deeper, some--like that fool at the Dutton--threw out a hand in desperation...
...clinging to anything that could give them hope.
No matter what the consequences.
NO!
The cruel loss to an unknowing world.
MY NOVEL!
I WORKED ON THAT FOR SEVEN YEARS!
A loss that could never go unpunished.
I... I KEPT MEANING TO BACK IT UP...

YOU ARE SO DEAD!
It all fit perfectly, every minute detail fitting into the larger picture with an audible snap.
The ascent to hitherto unscalable heights...
GOTHAMITE
UP CLOSE
by Mel Staines
Followed by the tragic yet inescapable slip...
And a brilliant life and career is cut down in its prime, smothered by fate--
--and clods who wouldn't recognize genius if it walked up to 'em and bit 'em.

Amateurs. Poseurs. Wannabes.
THE RARE BOOKS... THEY'RE ALL...
SSES

Jerks.
YOU MIGHT SAY I MADE MY MARK ON ALL OF THEM.
NO ONE WILL EVER FORGET ME OR WHAT I DID. I'M ONE OF THE IMMORTALS NOW.

AND MY WORDS... ONCE I PUT THEM BACK TOGETHER, THEY'RE DESTINED TO STAND THE TEST OF TIME.
YOU'VE READ SOME OF THEM. YOU KNOW.
HA
HA HA
HA HA

YES. TOO MANY WORDS, TOO LITTLE SUBSTANCE. YOU'RE A HACK, MISS STAINES.
YOUR VANDALISM MAY BE REMEMBERED... BUT YOUR WRITING WILL NEVER BE MORE THAN A FOOTNOTE.
The End

CHAPTER 6: DEATHTRAP A-GO-GO

ROBIN

ROBIN

AN ABANDONED WAREHOUSE SOMEWHERE IN GOTHAM CITY...
NUTS! ALMOST MIDNIGHT! THEY'VE GOT US IN A TIGHT SPOT, BATMAN--FAIR, SQUARE AND DEAD TO RIGHTS! IT'S BEEN COOL WORKING WITH YA, BUT THIS...THIS LOOKS LIKE THE END, MY FRIEND!
YOU THINK THIS IS A TIGHT SPOT? NOT EVEN CLOSE.
BATMAN AND HIS TENSE SIDEKICK ROBIN IN...
DEATHTRAP A-GO-GO!
GABE SORIA WRITER
DEAN HASPIEL ARTIST
NICK J. NAP-LETTERER • ZYLONOL-COLORIST
HARVEY RICHARDS-ASST. EDITOR • JOAN HILTY-EDITOR
BATMAN CREATED BY BOB KANE

HECK YEAH, I THINK THIS IS A TIGHT SPOT--I'M GONNA DIE AND I'VE NEVER EVEN SHAVED!
I'M WORKING ON FREEING US. RELAX.
YOU'RE A DETECTIVE, AREN'T YOU? WELL, DETECT THIS: WE ARE ABOUT TO CROAK!
THE BIG SPLITSKI!
BATMAN ZIGGED WHEN HE SHOULD HAVE ZAGGED.
ROBIN TOO FAST TO LIVE, TOO YOUNG TO DIE.
THE UNQUIET SLEEP OF THE AGES!
THE E-TICKET RIDE TO ETERNITY!
ROBIN, YOU HAVE TO PUT THE SITUATION IN PERSPECTIVE. DEATHTRAPS LIKE THIS ARE A PART OF THE JOB, AND TRUST ME--I'VE SEEN MUCH WORSE.
WORSE THAN THIS?

CROC COULD NEVER HAVE IMAGINED THAT AS A TEENAGER, I ONCE SPENT A SEASON IN A ROADSIDE CARNIVAL IN FLORIDA WRESTLING ALLIGATORS.

YOU WRESTLED ALLIGATORS? IN FLORIDA? IN A CARNIVAL?!

I WRESTLED ALLIGATORS. IN FLORIDA. IN A CARNIVAL. AND I WAS GOOD AT IT.

I'LL BET YOU WERE.

OR THE TIME I WAS RUNNING THROUGH A WHEAT FIELD ON THE OUTSKIRTS OF GOTHAM WITH THE PENGUIN DOGGING MY EVERY STEP IN HIS "BYE-BI-BIRD-PLANE"...
"BYE BI-BIRD-PLANE"?! THAT'S TERRIBLE! WHAT A CORNBALL! WAS HE TRYING TO KILL YOU WITH LAUGHTER?
MACHINE GUNS.
OH.

HOW APPROPRIATE THAT YOU SHOULD MENTION DYING LAUGHING. ONCE, THE JOKER IMPRISONED ME IN A CAR FILLED WITH *INFLATABLE PUNCHING-BAG CLOWNS.*
WHY DIDN'T YOU JUST POP THE CLOWNS?
THEY WERE INFLATED WITH THE JOKER'S *LAUGHING GAS.*
HAW!
URK! HOW'D YOU CHEAT CERTAIN DEATH *THAT* TIME?
THAT PARTICULAR MAKE OF CLOWN CAR HAD A VERY WEAK WINDSHIELD, AND I HAVE A VERY HARD HEAD. WHAT DOES A HARD HEAD PLUS A WEAK WINDSHIELD EQUAL?
A FREAKIN' *HEADACHE.*
A *WAY OUT,* ROBIN.
RIGHT. A *WAY OUT.*

I HAD TO USE MY HEAD IN A DIFFERENT WAY WHEN THE MAD HATTER HAD ME AT THE MERCY OF HIS INSIDIOUS "DE-CAP-ITATOR." HE WAS OBVIOUSLY NEVER A BOY SCOUT...
WHY?
HE'S A SKILLED HABERDASHER, BUT HIS KNOT-TYING SKILLS ARE POOR.
MENACED BY A KILLER HAT--ARE YOU SURE THIS WASN'T A NIGHTMARE BROUGHT ON BY ALFRED'S "SPECIAL" MEATLOAF? I MEAN, TALK ABOUT DEATHTRAPS!

NO, ROBIN--
I DON'T BELIEVE
ALFRED'S MEATLOAF
HAS CAUSED ME TO
HALLUCINATE DEADLY
PERIL LATELY.

WELL,
MAYBE NOT
YOU...

BUT HEY--YOU'RE
NOT GOING TO TELL
ALFRED I SAID THAT,
RIGHT?
NO, I WON'T
TELL ALFRED.
AFTER ALL, WHEN
AM I GOING TO HAVE
THE CHANCE?
RIGHT.
WE'RE NOT GOING
ANYWHERE.
OR SO YOU
THINK.
OR SO YOU
SAY.

ARE YOU
GOING TO
ALLOW ME TO
CONTINUE MY
STORY?
I'M ALL
EARS.
WELL THEN, LET
ME TELL YOU ABOUT THE
SCARECROW'S HOUSE
OF HORRORS...

ANOTHER DEATHTRAP?
YOU HAVE NO IDEA.

WOW. **COOL.** ASIDE FROM THE WHOLE *"INSTANT DEATH AWAITING YOU AROUND EVERY CORNER"* THING.
DEADLY AS IT WAS, IT WAS **ENTERTAINING.** SCARECROW'S A CREATIVE SOUL, AND I TOLD HIM THAT HE WAS WASTING HIS TIME TRYING TO KILL ME. HE SHOULD BE DESIGNING AMUSEMENT PARK RIDES. BUT IT'S IN ONE EAR AND OUT THE OTHER WITH CRIMINALS.
THAT BRINGS UP AN INTERESTING QUESTION, ACTUALLY.
YES?

MONEY.
MONEY?

YEAH, MONEY. WHERE DO THESE GUYS GET ALL THE MONEY TO **DO** THIS STUFF?

THEY **STEAL** IT, ROBIN.

OKAY, THEY STEAL IT. BUT IT'S NOT LIKE IT STOPS THERE.

WHAT DO YOU MEAN?

THINK ABOUT IT. THEY GET MONEY BY, SAY, LOOTING GOTHAM NATIONAL BANK, OR STEALING THE CROWN JEWELS OF ZAMUNDA FROM THE GOTHAM MUSEUM, OR WHATEVER.
ASSUMING WE DON'T STOP THEM.
ASSUMING WE DON'T STOP THEM. MOST CROOKS WOULD BE SATISFIED WITH THE MONEY. BUT THESE GUYS, ONCE THEY'VE GOT THE MONEY, THEY HAVE TO CONCEIVE A ***DEATHTRAP***...
RIGHT.

THEY HAVE TO ***BUDGET*** IT...
CORRECT.
SOIL
SOIL

THEY HAVE TO ***BUILD*** IT...
OF COURSE.

AND THEN, ONCE ALL THAT'S DONE, THEY HAVE TO LURE YOU ***INTO*** IT.
YES.

WELL?
"WELL", WHAT?
WELL, DOESN'T THAT SEEM A LITTLE...***CRAZY*** TO YOU? IF YOU ASK ME, THAT'S A LOT OF MONEY, TIME AND EFFORT JUST TO GET YOUR JAW SOCKED AND THROWN INTO ARKHAM ASYLUM!

OF COURSE IT'S CRAZY, ROBIN. THESE ARE ***MENTALLY UNBALANCED CRIMINALS*** WE'RE DEALING WITH.

NOT SO LONG AGO, CLAYFACE TRIED TO MAKE ME A PERMANENT PART OF AN ENORMOUS COFFEE MUG. IT MIGHT HAVE WORKED--HAD HE NOT USED AN INFERIOR, SLOW-DRYING CLAY THAT I WAS ABLE TO PULL FREE FROM AT THE LAST MOMENT.
HUH. YOU'D FIGURE--HIM BEING MADE O' CLAY--THAT HE'D KNOW BETTER THAN THAT, RIGHT?
WELL, YOUR TYPICAL CRIMINAL IS, BY AND LARGE, CRIMINALLY FOOLISH.
AND IT SOUNDS LIKE THEY CRIMINALLY CUT CORNERS ON COSTS, TOO...

AND ONE HOT JULY DAY, MR. FREEZE INTRODUCED BRAINFREEZE, A SINISTER NEW FLAVOR OF ICE CREAM, TO THE STREETS OF GOTHAM.
MMM. TASTY.
HARDLY. ONE LICK, AND A PERSON WAS UNDER FREEZE'S COMPLETE MENTAL DOMINATION, SUSCEPTIBLE TO HIS EVERY SUGGESTION.
BRAIN FREEZE
I BET HIS FIRST SUGGESTION WAS "PLEASE KILL BATMAN FOR ME, WOULDJA?"
EXACTLY. BUT WHAT HE DIDN'T PLAN ON WAS BEING HIS OWN ANTIDOTE. AFTER ALL, WHAT KILLS THE DESIRE FOR ICE CREAM QUICKER THAN A FREEZING WINTER'S DAY?
I WOULD'VE JUST DOUSED 'EM IN HOT CHOCOLATE SYRUP--BUT THAT'S ME!

ONCE, TWO-FACE OFFERED ME A CHOICE BETWEEN ONE OF TWO DOORS...
BUT THERE WAS A CATCH.
OF COURSE. THE CATCH WAS, BOTH DOORS LED TO A CERTAIN, PAINFUL DEATH. ALL I HAD TO DO WAS CHOOSE.
SO DID YA JUST DIVE RIGHT IN ONE?
NOT AT ALL. TWO-FACE'S MISTAKE WAS OFFERING ME A CHOICE BETWEEN DEATHS--AND I CHOSE NEITHER.
2
AND OPENED UP A BIG BAT-CAN OF WHUP-...
LANGUAGE, ROBIN.

THEN THERE WAS RIDDLER AND HIS FONDNESS FOR GAME SHOWS. IT WAS ME VERSUS TWO UNLUCKY CITIZENS OF GOTHAM. THE PUNISHMENT FOR ANSWERING A QUESTION WRONG--10,000 VOLTS. THE PUNISHMENT FOR NOT ANSWERING AT ALL--20,000 VOLTS.
SHOCKING! TRUTH OR DARE
I HAD NO CHOICE. I BUZZED ON EVERY QUESTION AND ANSWERED EVERY ONE WRONG. I TOOK EVERY SINGLE SHOCK UNTIL THE RIDDLER CAME OVER TO GLOAT OVER MY BODY...
YOU SPRANG BACK TO LIFE AND CLOCKED HIM, NATURALLY. BUT...20,000 VOLTS? REPEATEDLY? THAT SOUNDS LIKE A JOB FOR...
...A LITTLE ELECTRICAL KNOWLEDGE. THE RIDDLER SHOULD HAVE KNOWN THAT THE BATSUIT IS HEAVILY INSULATED AGAINST JUST THIS SORT OF THING. VOLTAGE MEANS NOTHING WITHOUT THE AMPS TO BACK IT UP.

NO KIDDING. HOW GOES IT WITH THE WHOLE *"FREEING US"* STRATEGY, BY THE WAY?
FUNNY THAT YOU SHOULD MENTION THAT...***THERE.***

YOU ***GOT*** IT! ROCK AND ***ROLL!***

SO: WHAT HAVE WE LEARNED?

ONE: YOUR ARCH-ENEMIES ARE, TO A FAULT, ARTS AND CRAFTS NUTS. ***TWO:*** YOU HAVE AN EXTREMELY HARD HEAD. ***THREE:*** DON'T SWEAT THE DEATHTRAPS.

EXACTLY.
I SAY WE GO AHEAD AND PUT A HURTIN' ON THESE SUCKERS. CAN YOU DIG IT?

NOT MUCH OF A STRATEGY, MY YOUNG FRIEND, BUT YES, I CAN "DIG IT."
AWWW YEAH-- I KNEW THAT YOU COULD!
THE EVER-LOVIN' DEADLY END!

ROBIN

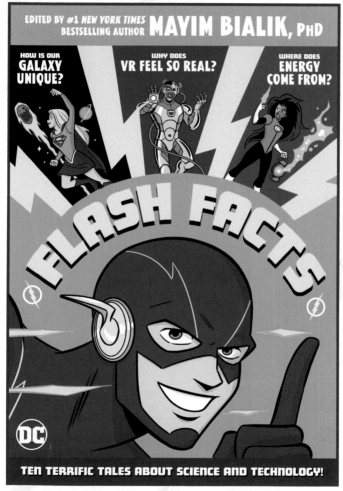

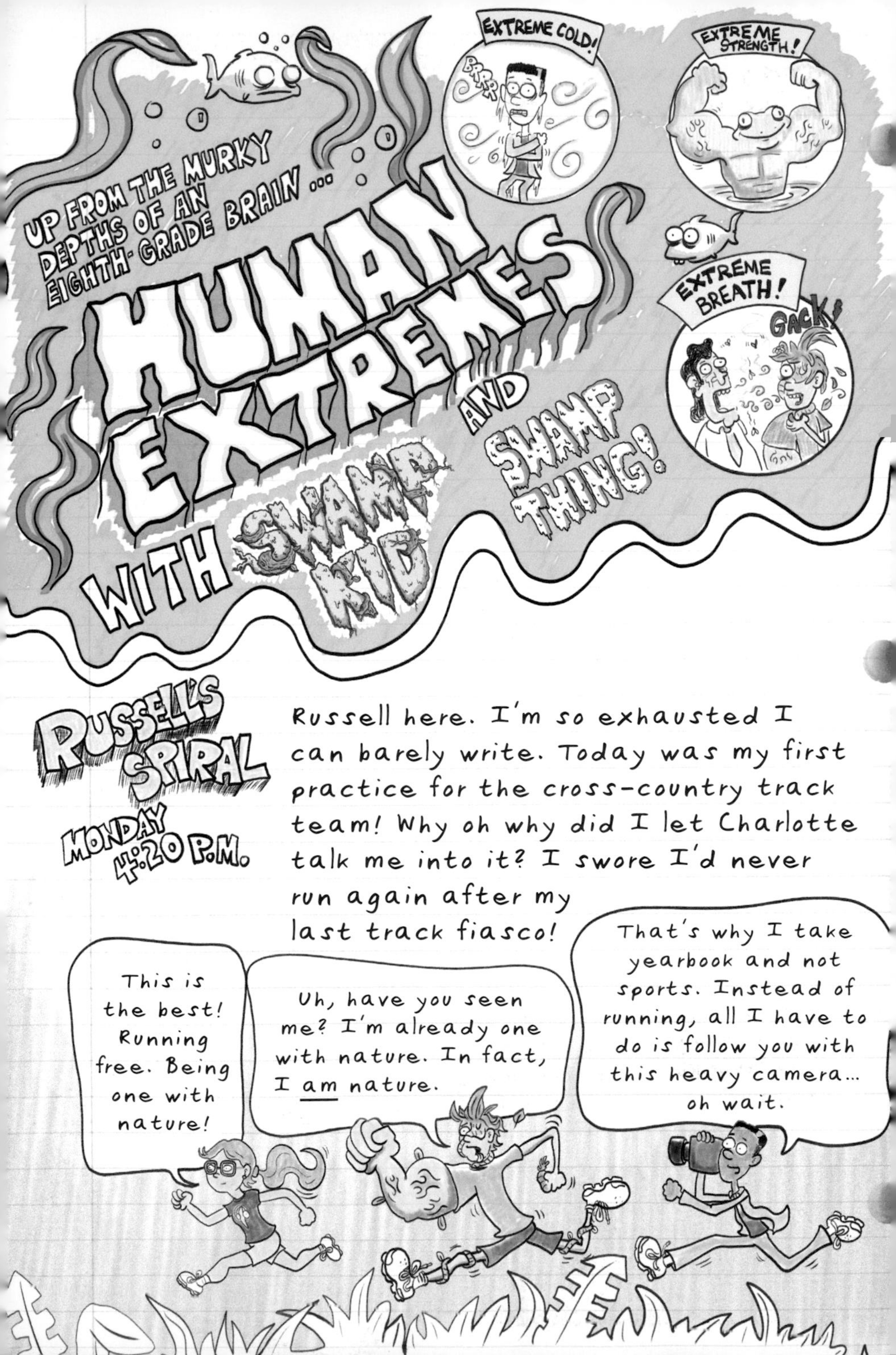

UP FROM THE MURKY DEPTHS OF AN EIGHTH-GRADE BRAIN...
HUMAN EXTREMES WITH SWAMP KID AND SWAMP THING!
EXTREME COLD!
BRRR
EXTREME STRENGTH!
EXTREME BREATH!
GACK!
RUSSELL'S SPIRAL
MONDAY 4:20 P.M.
Russell here. I'm so exhausted I can barely write. Today was my first practice for the cross-country track team! Why oh why did I let Charlotte talk me into it? I swore I'd never run again after my last track fiasco!
This is the best! Running free. Being one with nature!
Uh, have you seen me? I'm already one with nature. In fact, I am nature.
That's why I take yearbook and not sports. Instead of running, all I have to do is follow you with this heavy camera... oh wait.

It may not look like it but this bod was actually built for endurance running.
Motivational frog
Aerodynamic carrot finger
Giant arm to help maintain balance
Strong walnut-sized calves
Who are we kidding? This is grueling!
Somebody call an ambulance! Or better yet, the cemetery. Tell my parents I love them and donate my foliage to science.
Looks like you boys just reached the lactate threshold!
Tell me about it. I can barely handle milkshakes anymore.
Not lactose intolerance. Lactate threshold!
LACTATE:
-Produced when the body turns food into energy.
-Really increases during vigorous exercise!

Normally, your body absorbs lactate, but if you're overdoing it, your cells can't keep up and the lactate starts to stockpile. That can lead to uncomfortable consequences...
BURNING MUSCLES
EXHAUSTION
EVEN
BARF
You've hit your lactate threshold and your body's saying, "Gimme a rest why don'tcha!"
If only I could increase my lactate threshold.
Funny you should say that. Ultramarathoners do it all the time.
ULTRA MARATHONERS
INTENSE SHORT WORKOUTS
They train in short, super intense bursts, gradually increasing the duration and the intensity.
It helps build up their endurance so they can run longer and harder without crossing the threshold. One even ran a hundred miles in less than twelve hours!
Flash Fact!
Um, okayyy?

Charlotte's extreme running lesson was interrupted by a strange dark cloud that came over us and blotted out the sun!
Looks like a gully-washer is coming, as my granny would say!
That isn't a rain cloud!
But it sure is frigid! Let's get outta here! Brrrrr!
We headed indoors fast!
TUES. 8:55 A.M.
On the bus, headed to school. The mystery cloud is still hovering over the town. And it's cold! Way cold for springtime.
HOUMA BAYOU MIDDLE SCHOOL
To be continued in FLASH FACTS Coming Spring 2021!

Discover how I went from pond scum to hero!
THE SECRET
SWAMP KID
Hi, I'm Russell and I'm just a normal kid. Except I've got algae for hair, a tree trunk for a right arm, and a frog as one of my friends.
THE SECRET SPIRAL OF SWAMP KID
BY KIRK SCROGGS
Written & Illustrated by
KIRK SCROGGS
DC
ON SALE NOW
A new graphic nove
for kid
™ & © DC